Empress
of
Misfortune

a novella based on
Cantiga 5
of the *Cantigas de Santa Maria*
of Alfonso X, *el Sabio*

J. K. KNAUSS

Açedrex Publishing
2022

Empress of Misfortune

J. K. Knauss

2022

ISBN 978-1-937291-77-8 (e-book)

ISBN 979-8-840983-10-2 (softcover)

Açedrex Publishing

Reading is the noblest pastime.

Zamora

Acedrex.com

HISTORICAL NOTE

Empress of Misfortune adapts the plot of *Cantiga* 5 of the *Cantigas de Santa Maria* into a novella. *Cantiga* 5 survives in the To, E, and *Códice rico* manuscripts. For a description of the *Cantigas de Santa Maria*, the greatest collection of miracles assembled in the Middle Ages, and Alfonso X, *el Sabio*'s musical, poetic, and artistic legacy, please see the introduction to *Our Lady's Troubadour* (Encircle Publications, 2021).

I've conceived this novella as a companion to *Our Lady's Troubadour*. I didn't want to upset the ten-*cantiga* structure of that collection. Since the empress's story is so different and so much longer, I decided it could stand on its own, slightly apart from the others, but hopefully on the same shelf.

This tale of the chaste empress was wildly popular in the Middle Ages. No fewer than ten manuscripts of the twelfth and thirteenth centuries from France, England, and Italy could've served as the inspiration for the version that appears in the *Cantigas de Santa Maria*.

Cantiga 5 is the fourth-longest *cantiga*, with 26 stanzas, and its length is due to it being a thirteenth-century Spanish poetic/musical example of a Byzantine novel. A medieval literary genre that revived a tradition from Ancient Greece, a Byzantine novel includes complex and often surprising plot twists, and the heroes usually travel all over the Mediterranean. I've been delighted by several other Spanish works in this genre, including the thirteenth-century *Book of Apollonius* and Miguel de Cervantes's *The Trials of Persiles and Segismunda*, and always hoped to write one myself.

I find the fantastical aspects of this genre especially appealing. All of the *Cantigas de Santa*

Maria have a strong folkloric feel, but *Cantiga 5* in particular calls to mind a fairy tale, with its idealized nobility and unrelenting tests of fortitude. The plot's existence outside of space and time, which looks like an unapologetic disregard for realism or historical accuracy, remind me of that masterpiece that first alerted me to the Middle Ages, *The Princess Bride*.

In spite of the freedom afforded by the genre, this story still conforms to King Alfonso X's conceptions of his ideal kingdom, full of virtue, fairness, justice, and piety. In the empress's case, it just takes an especially long time to get to them.

Cantiga 5 has two pages of illustrations in the *Códice rico*, and photos of them are included at the end of the story. They inspired many of the details in a few of the scenes you're about to read.

I.

Empress Beatriz, the most beautiful woman in Rome and indeed the entire empire, sat in a gilded armchair on a platform surrounded by noble ladies. Her friends and attendants rested on embroidered velvet pillows, doing needlework of all sorts and listening intently as the empress read to them from a small book of prayers to St. Mary, Mother of God.

The book's multicolored jewels glinted in the bright light from an open colonnade looking over the city with its hills, forums, and temples and the plain beneath a cloudless sky, as bright blue as the Virgin's cloak.

A knock interrupted her reading. The empress looked up as a guard cranked open the heavy carved oak door just wide enough to see one of the emperor's pages waiting. Beatriz couldn't remember the emperor ever having sent a page to her quarters before. His eyes wide, the page inhaled deeply and smoothed his hair around his ears. A young maid who had only attended the empress for a month abandoned her embroidery to keep the young man from barging inside.

"I have a message from Emperor Antoninus," the page told her.

The girl made a gesture and the door opened fully under the power of both of the guards. The empress watched the page cross the room and barely suppressed a chuckle. He was entranced by all he saw: an enormous bedstead with rich green sheets and enough pillows for all the attendants, if only it weren't for the empress's private use, and tastefully decorated trunks and tables storing the empress's gowns and jewelry. The page's awe at the things that surrounded her every day was delightful. She supposed he hadn't yet seen the inside of her beloved husband's quarters, which made her room look like a hovel.

He knelt at the edge of the platform and doffed his cap, keeping his gaze appropriately away from Beatriz's eyes.

"Your Imperial Majesty, the emperor requests

your presence at once. He awaits you in the throne room."

The empress stood and handed her treasured book to the lady at her right. "Very well," she said to the page. "I would not delay complying with my husband's wishes. You may accompany me to the throne room."

Beatriz glided through corridors on embroidered silk slippers. The page hurried to keep up. She looked across at him, and he averted his gaze.

Antoninus had always treated Beatriz with respect, which cleared the way for mutual affection, and finally lasting love. She had long been accustomed to being consulted on important matters of state and wondered at such a sudden summons.

"Did the emperor say what this is about?" the empress asked.

"No, Your Imperial Majesty, but there is someone new with him. If you permit me, I'll wager it has something to do with the newcomer."

Normally, the emperor and the empress received foreign dignitaries together, so if the stranger was someone important, it was highly uncustomary that Beatriz hadn't heard about the visit long beforehand. She must find out who he was and why she hadn't been prepared for his arrival.

"Thank you," she told the page. Hurry was no excuse for mistreatment of the staff, but she picked up her pace, not bothering to check whether he kept up or fell behind.

Guards armed with pikestaffs opened the equally decorated and heavy doors of the throne room to the empress. They knelt as she floated past.

The empress had expected a quantity of noblemen, advisors, and servants sufficient to make the cavernous room look small. But before the gilded throne backed with velvet drapery in imperial purple with gold embroidery stood only her adored husband and his guest.

The visitor didn't look especially foreign. In fact, he looked much like the emperor, dressed sumptuously, with the same eyes and the same broad shoulders. He might've been the emperor himself several years ago. Beatriz curtsied at a respectful distance and then drew nearer to Antoninus.

"Good husband, who is our guest? Why was I not prepared for his arrival?"

"Darling Beatriz, this is my beloved brother, Felix."

The visitor grinned and bowed before the empress.

"Welcome, young Felix." Beatriz held out her

hand. The visitor took it with an excess of force and kissed it indelicately. The empress looked to her husband. "I've never met him before. I know he lives far away." That explained his strange hat, at least. "What brings him to us now?"

"I was fostered at the court of Constantinople to guarantee good relations across the Middle Sea." He winked. "I'll let my brother explain why I'm here now."

Antoninus took her hands and looked into her eyes. "I've called you here because news has come of a crusade to take Jerusalem. I must join the fighters there and take my army."

"You would leave me in Rome by myself?" She squeezed his hands. She couldn't imagine life in the palace without him. So many emissaries to welcome, so many servants to take care of, so many nights alone. "Please don't do this, husband."

"I don't make this decision lightly. Of course, I would rather stay here with you and my people. But I must make good on the promise I made to the Pope. And I know I can trust you to take care of the Roman people and rule over them wisely while I'm gone."

She wrenched away, and Felix startled.

"And this brother?" Beatriz demanded. "Did you

bring him here so that I wouldn't make a scene?"

Antoninus brought Felix forward by the shoulders, presenting him to the empress. "He'll be good company to you in my absence. Although Felix is my brother, receive him as my son and be a mother to him."

And now she had to take care of some stranger as if she hadn't already done her motherly duty bearing the emperor's true children and raising them to forge great political alliances. Felix looked to her like a whipped puppy seeking forgiveness. His gaze darted all over her to the point that she thought she felt it on her skin. They must have strange customs in Constantinople. There was no nobility in his bearing, and she wondered that someone such as he could be related to her Antoninus.

"Do not hesitate to chastise him, for in so doing you show me great honor," said the emperor. It was as if he'd read her mind. Perhaps she could educate this Felix as she had her children, and when the emperor returned, his brother would be a credit to the family.

"Please tell me you won't be gone long. I—and your people—will miss you so much." Beatriz refrained from embracing him only because Felix was still staring at them.

"I'll return as soon as I've fulfilled my obligations to the Pope."

The empress heard practiced diplomacy in her husband's answer, but looking into his eyes, she knew he had every intention of returning to her. Beatriz kissed Antoninus on the cheek daintily, then set her jaw and arranged a room for Felix many twisting passageways away from her own. That night, Antoninus stayed with her and didn't leave until one of the guards came to tell him it was time to go to the port.

Beatriz couldn't accompany the emperor to the port of Ostia, for Rome was now her responsibility, but she embraced him as he prepared to step into the imperial carriage and didn't let go of his hand until the horses pulled away. Flanked by imperial guards, she should've felt secure. But she watched the carriage rolling farther into the distance, long after it rounded a bend, long after the dust settled, thinking that perhaps she might never move from that spot until Antoninus returned.

Finally, she whispered "Ave Maria, gratia plena," and headed back to the palace, the guards close behind.

The impression that Antoninus, years younger, was welcoming her back to the palace put a lump in her throat until the man came into closer focus. It was Felix who waited at the gatehouse like a faithful dog. Beatriz looked at him askance as she entered, giving the slightest nod. He fell into step behind her, so she whirled around.

"Felix, I'll see you at supper."

"Of course, Your Imperial Majesty." He made an exaggerated bow and stayed behind as Beatriz led the guards to the emperor's study.

The room, lined with shelves full of scrolls, loose pages, and bound volumes, had a single window, which was shuttered. One of the guards moved to open it, but Beatriz stayed his hand. A scent of musk, sweet wine, and resin lingered in the air. It would not do to let this memory of the emperor fly out on the breeze.

Advisors came and went. Some told Beatriz about the emissaries who were due to visit court. Another gave her a list of monarchs who were headed to the crusade with Antoninus. Beatriz dictated letter after letter to the scribe, explaining the situation and enquiring as to whether the country in question would prefer to wait for the emperor's return. She signed each letter "I, the Empress" with her own hand. When she suspected that a country's king had left his queen in charge, as Antoninus had Beatriz, she added some lines about getting along without their husbands, even though they missed them very much, and invited regular correspondence to keep their spirits up while the crusade lasted. She composed personal missives to her daughter and son, telling them how proud she was of them and their diplomatic success in France and Germany, but also how she wished they could all be in Rome together. The scribe waited silently for the empress to dry her lonely tears.

A plate of fruit appeared on the desk in the afternoon, just when she was thinking she might have to lie down for a while. She laid the latest letter on the stack to be sent and absently reached for a grape. As the refreshing juices burst in her mouth, her gaze wandered up to the man who had brought the tray. Felix.

Beatriz startled, and stood up from the desk to mask it.

"Isn't there anything I can help you with, Your Imperial Majesty?"

Her throat was dry from dictating and with the emotions of the day. She must maintain her dignity. "No, Felix. Well, there is something that would relieve a burden for me."

"Anything," he said, clasping his hands.

"Please see to the evening meal. Arrange the menu with the cooks, check that the servants are fed, and consult with them about the number of guests and courses."

Felix furrowed his brow at what he surely considered a woman's task. Then his face brightened slowly, as if a priest lit each taper in succession along the apse of his countenance.

"It shall be as you wish, Your Imperial Majesty."

He left the study bowing, and Beatriz forgot about him. Another scribe came to relieve the first, but there was no one to replace the empress.

Hours later, she slumped to her quarters, too tired to speak with her ladies, who dressed her for supper in a velvet gown with jewels that would sparkle in the candlelight.

"Anyone at dinner will be too dazzled to notice the emperor is gone," said the youngest damsel. Beatriz looked at her forlornly, wishing she could trade places with her.

"Chin up, Your Imperial Majesty," said another, more experienced lady. "You can do this last thing, and then come back here and rest."

Beatriz clasped her hands with gratitude. She wasn't sure she was capable of entertaining guests after such a long day, but at least her ladies believed in her. She stood up straight and practiced her gracious gestures as she made her way to the dining chamber.

The room was ablaze with candles, each branch of twenty chandeliers glowing warmly, yet they illuminated no people. Beatriz took a seat in Antoninus's place at the head of the table and gazed along its length. Only one other place was set. Her heart felt lighter; she didn't have to entertain dignitaries after all. But of course, the other place setting, right next to hers, could belong to no one else but Felix.

The emperor's brother strode into the room, admiring the excessive illumination he must've ordered. His gaze alighted on Beatriz, and he slid into his chair without looking at anything else.

The entire day—watching her husband ride away, working so hard and talking so much—had exhausted the empress. Could she make it through a supper with this strange man when all she wanted was to collapse?

"Good evening," she murmured.

Felix nodded, the candles sparking in his eyes. A page ladled soup into their bowls and exited again. Beatriz tore at the bread fretfully.

"I don't wonder at your sorrow, Your Imperial

Majesty," said Felix, "for my brother is all an emperor should be, and must also fulfill his duties as a husband to you as well. But consider that I may have some little part of Antoninus in me. We were born of the same mother and father, after all."

He caught her hand before she could take up her spoon. "And if you deign to make use of any part of me in my brother's absence, you will make me the happiest man in the empire, for I love you with all my heart. I will serve you faithfully until the day Antoninus returns."

His hand on hers seemed to cover the hole that had opened in Beatriz's heart as the carriage had driven away. Felix offered a bandage for her open wound. But it was her duty to endure the pain of Antoninus's absence until he and he alone could apply the true remedy.

"How can you suggest something like this?" The empress tore her hand away. "The emperor probably hasn't even sailed yet. His bed is still warm, and you would lie down in his place."

"No one ever need know. It will be our secret." He stood and pressed against the arm of her chair, looming over her. "I don't want his power, only his wife."

The empress looked up at eyes that seemed to

devour her. "He's your brother. I'm your brother's wife. I'm to be as a mother to you, no more."

Felix's impassioned breath cascaded down her neck. "Come now, Beatriz. I can tell you like me. Don't deny it." He lay his hand on her shoulder and his thumb caressed her collarbone.

"Your face is handsome, but your soul is twisted like the wiles of the Devil." She swept her soup bowl to the floor, and the thick green liquid coated his gold-embroidered tunic.

"You'll pay for denying me!"

His hands enclosed her throat. As she grabbed them, he dragged her to the floor, upsetting her chair. Her knee landed in the empty soup bowl, and then he dragged her by the hair. The empress kicked at the air, but couldn't slow his progress. She let out a scream that began weak and dry but grew louder and heartier with her rage.

Two imperial guards charged through the door and pulled Felix off the empress before she knew what was happening.

The scoundrel kicked and struggled against them, so Beatriz had to find her bearings and stand without their help. She observed the soup on her skirt and the jewels from her necklace scattered on the floor. What was she supposed to do without Antoninus? All she could think was that she wanted to lie down in her bed and forget that this day had happened.

"Your Imperial Majesty, what shall we do with him?" asked one of the guards.

"Unhand me this instant!" Felix growled. "How dare you lay hands on the emperor's brother?"

"How dare you?" Beatriz asked Felix, summoning the calm with which Antoninus would've welcomed emissaries from Germany. "How dare you, the emperor's brother, dishonor his house and his empire?" She stared into his eyes, hoping he felt as helpless as she had at the table. "Antoninus told me I should castigate you as a mother would a son, but I see there is no correcting you. You've strayed too far from the straight road."

She stood back and addressed the guard. "Throw him in the dungeon. Do not bring him food or water without my permission."

Felix shouted and struggled, but the scandal was muffled as soon as the guards wrestled him out the door. Beatriz righted the chair and sat down, her face in her hands. The door creaked open behind her, and soft footsteps came close. When she opened her eyes, the page who had ladled the soup had placed a platter of steaming chickpeas in thick sauce on the table.

Antoninus had once dined on chickpeas on the

advice of a physician when they were trying to conceive their first prince of the empire. "This is what he had the cooks make?" said the empress.

"There's also a goose. It's just finishing up, Your Imperial Majesty."

"Let the household have the goose. I'm going to eat some of these chickpeas and retire for the night."

"As you wish, Your Imperial Majesty." The page bowed and left her.

Beatriz spooned the hearty meal into her mouth, paying little attention to where the sauce splattered. The sustenance calmed her, and after finishing the jug of red wine, she felt strong enough to face her aggressor. She removed a taper from one of the candelabras and descended the dark staircase, receiving obeisance from each of the guards she met along the way. The last one hesitated to make way.

"Your Imperial Majesty, are you certain you want to see that man?"

"Yes," she said with a confidence she didn't feel. "Please open the door."

As she brought the taper nearer, Beatriz saw that Felix was shackled by the foot to the exterior wall. He couldn't reach her like that, but his eyes glinted at her with frustration and desire.

"Felix, I don't want to have to leave you here." It

was true. Beatriz didn't want to have to explain the situation to Antoninus. "Are you ready to be let out?"

"Only so I may occupy your bed, Beatriz." He chomped at the air, and Beatriz was sure he would devour her if only he had the chance.

She left the cell, and when the guard locked the door again, she put her face to the small, barred window. "You may have the same mother and father, but you are not and never will be anything like Antoninus."

She returned to her room without altering the instructions to leave him hungry and thirsty. The following day, after receiving emissaries from Tangier and writing a decree to prohibit emptying excrement buckets into the main thoroughfare, she traveled below to check on her criminal brother-in-law. This time, she asked his prostrate form, "Have you had enough?"

"Yes," he croaked. "Please let me out."

She motioned to the guard, and he brought the key to the shackle. He couldn't see to unlock it, so Beatriz brought her taper near. Once his leg was free, Felix stood and lunged at Beatriz in one motion, knocking the candle to the ground and snuffing it.

The empress screamed in the dark against the chaos of arms and legs all over her. Suddenly, the guard's enormous hand was pressing on her shoulder for leverage to pry Felix off. Then, she was scooped into his arms and alighted near the torch in the wall outside the cell. As she caught her breath, she saw another guard secure Felix to the wall and close the cell door. They stood looking at her with concern.

"Let him have bread and water, but only bread and water, until I say differently." She took the second guard's candle and headed up the stairs, wiping tears on her sleeves all the way up.

II.

Over the next few months, Beatriz checked on Felix weekly. Seeing that he never surprised her with a change of heart, and she had so many affairs to attend to, she relaxed his food rations, but limited the unpleasant visits to once a month. At Easter the following year, she was busy coordinating feasts and processions, and didn't see Felix until May. Her ladies told her she should give up on him and have him executed. But she was already going to have enough trouble explaining why he was in the dungeon when Antoninus came back. How could she justify killing the emperor's brother while he was away?

She couldn't let go of the idea that Felix was the blood relative of her Antoninus and must have some shred of redeemability, but with one thing and another, she became distracted and the visits ceased entirely, although she never made the decision.

One afternoon, Beatriz had finally managed to get the empire's affairs in order long enough for her to spend a few hours the way she had been accustomed: reading prayers of the Blessed Virgin to her ladies in the privacy of her chamber. The prayer book's stiff pages felt like home in her hands, and the gold leaf of the capitals shone as she turned them. A warm sun through the colonnade leant its glow to the ladies as they worked quietly with their needles. In the calm clicking, Beatriz felt harmony respire through the room.

But again, an unexpected knock at the door. It was the same page who had interrupted them two-and-a-half years previously.

"Letters, Your Imperial Majesty," he gasped. "Letters from the emperor! Sent by special courier. His horse died at the gate from the effort."

A maiden snatched the folded parchment from the breathless man and handed it to the empress, who took it after setting down the jeweled book. Beatriz scanned the contents and read them aloud.

"My dear wife,

"We were in Acre for two-and-a-half years, but

by the grace of God, we have won it, and it is now the capital of the Kingdom of Jerusalem. It's time for me to return to my empire, and to your side, where I have remained always in my heart."

"The emperor is coming back!" shouted a lady, and the others followed suit.

Beatriz waited for them to calm down, thinking how fortunate it was that she had been able to protect the empire so well in Antoninus's absence. When he returned to the palace, he could surely find no fault with the way she'd handled all the affairs, foreign, domestic, and household.

"'We've had an uneventful crossing, and I'm writing to you at the port of Ostia.'" Beatriz's heart swelled. "He's not coming, he's already here." She needn't wait any longer, and she needn't hurry, because there was nothing to prepare. After all this time, all was finally well.

"'The imperial retinue is prepared. I will see you, my sweet bride, and Felix tomorrow.'"

The letters fell to the floor. The emperor mustn't return to find Felix rotting in the dungeon.

Beatriz stepped down from the platform, nearly tripping over her own slipper. Ladies cleared pillows and furniture from her path and the guards opened the door to her without need of words. She ran along the corridors and stumbled down the staircase. There seemed to be many more steps than before. Seeing only by the torches on the wall, she startled the guard at the cell door.

The man snapped to attention. "Your Imperial Majesty."

"Is he in there?" Beatriz saw nothing past the bars on the window.

"I think he's asleep, Your Imperial Majesty."

"The emperor is returning tomorrow." Beatriz held the words in her mouth with a mixture of hope and dread. "As soon as I leave here, you must release Felix." She removed the rings from both of her hands and poured them into the guard's. "Give him these and whatever else he requests within reason, so long as he leaves the palace by the back and never returns here again. I'll tell the emperor his brother disappeared two years ago and we suspect gambling debts to be a part of it."

She stared into the guard's eyes for a moment longer and found the sympathy she sought. "Please send word when it's done." She lifted her skirts and ascended the stairs deliberately so as not to return to her quarters as breathless as the page had been.

Reflexively smoothing her hair as the door cranked open, she entered saying, "Now, where was

I?" No matter how many pages she turned, however, she couldn't find that sense of calm that had flowed so freely before. The ladies' silence seemed distracted, and the clicking of their needles played on Beatriz's nerves. At last, just before supper, a messenger was admitted into the chamber.

"The prisoner was given a steed of his choosing from the stable and was seen to be riding fast away from Rome, Your Imperial Majesty."

Several sighs of relief echoed around the chamber. "Thank you very much," said Beatriz. "I'll be sure to tell the cooks to reward you at supper."

When the messenger was gone, so were her troubles. All that kept the empress awake that night were thoughts of Antoninus in her arms again.

Before dawn, Beatriz woke her personal maids to dress her and do her hair.

"What time will the emperor arrive?" wondered one of the maids.

"It's not clear," said Beatriz, "but I'm going to be ready."

When the mirror reflected an image of unsurpassable beauty and grace that Antoninus couldn't help but run to meet and kiss all over, Beatriz stepped lightly along the path to the gatehouse and waited, a permanent smile on her face.

One of the guards broke the anticipatory silence at midmorning. "Your Imperial Majesty, won't you even break your fast?"

"I couldn't keep anything down, thank you," she replied, never removing her gaze from the road. Every movement of every cart, donkey, hog, horseman, or pedestrian started her heart racing and her eyes darting, searching for signs of Antoninus's arrival. When the sun was at its highest, faint with hunger, Beatriz squinted at the movement far ahead, hardly expecting anything. Banners sprouted from the horizon to be followed by the horses of the imperial retinue's vanguard.

Beatriz forgot herself, picked up her skirts, and ran down the road. The procession halted so as not to trample her as she passed horses, footmen, and carts, searching for the emperor. At last, there he was, in the center of it all, atop an enormous black courser. His hair hung down, whiter than before, but Beatriz had expected some sort of change. She stretched her hand up, and it only reached the top of the saddle. Antoninus looked down at her and motioned to his guards. They helped him down.

When they were face to face, Beatriz didn't see the adoration she knew she must be showing him. Even that strangeness didn't prepare her for the strike across her face that nearly toppled her.

She planted her feet. "It is I, Beatriz, the empress, your loving and devoted wife," she said, touching her lip to find blood. "Don't you recognize me?"

"All too well," Antoninus growled. He gestured, and guards she didn't recognize grasped her by the arms. They must be prisoners, enemies captured in the Holy Land. "You are the harlot who bothered, cajoled, and pled with my brother, Felix, to lie with you in my absence. When he refused, you threw him in prison and left him there to rot, only to release him just before I arrived."

Beatriz appealed to his mercy, bowing as much as she could under the guards' grasp. "Who told you these lies? It's not true, it's the wrong way around…"

The liar stepped out from behind the emperor. Felix hadn't cut his hair or shaved his beard for two-and-a-half years, and that much had to do with Beatriz's justified actions. But he'd also torn his clothes and dirtied his face and hands, caking the filth under his cheekbones to appear more emaciated. He launched a grin at Beatriz, and his eyes sparkled with malice, just as they had in the dining room two-and-a-half years before.

"You must know I didn't leave my brother with you so you could shame my family in this way," said the emperor, the man who had welcomed her into his home and his heart. Then he spoke slowly with gestures so the guards would understand. "Take her into the forest and kill her. I don't care how."

Before she could protest again, the enormous hands of the two new guards were upon Beatriz. The crowd parted for the guards as they hadn't for the empress, so they were able to throw her across a horse and tie her to it with little resistance. She moved her wrists this way and that, and pulled at the rope at her ankles, but they were bound fast. Too soon, the horse was moving, and it was all she could do to breathe against the animal's ribs.

She listened to the guards' burbling, but their language was completely wild and made no sense. In a fraction of the time she'd waited at the gate for her love to return, they arrived in the middle of a forest the empress didn't recognize. When the horse stopped, Beatriz worked at the ropes again, but the guards cut her away from the mount and she stood before them, bound at hands and feet, unable to run.

Her only hope resided far above them and was watching everything. "St. Mary, Mother of God and protector of sinners, protect me, since I've done no wrong." She pressed her hands further together.

The two men looked her over in a ravenous way

she knew all too well from Felix. They spoke to each other, then, having made some kind of agreement, one reached for her collar and pulled as if to tear her dress away.

Beatriz screamed with all her might. The guard clapped his hand over her mouth and the sound faded into the treetops.

They toppled into fallen leaves and branches. She squeezed her eyes shut. "Ave Maria, Ave Maria, St. Mary, save me!" she said into his rough and sweaty palm even as she struggled against both men while they tried to undo the lacings at her sides.

She heard two grunts and opened her eyes to see that all the movement had stopped. The guards lay on the forest floor and a new man stood before her. He stooped to untie her wrists. The man wore an expensive velvet tunic, and his horse, a bit farther away, carried blazons of nobility.

"St. Mary's answer to my prayer," said Beatriz, massaging her chafed wrists.

The man laughed. "I'm Count Magnus, and I've done no more than common decency required. My lady, may I undo the bonds at your ankles?"

"Please do, kind count. I don't know how to thank you." Beatriz looked herself over. A few mendable tears in the fabric of her dress, and bruises would likely surface later.

When her ankles were free, he stood and offered his hand to help her stand. "My lady, may I ask who you are?"

Beatriz realized that she had nowhere to go, and didn't know where to find anything to eat. "I'm a pitiable, unfortunate woman in need of your aid. Perhaps you know where there's a convent or an abbey? I need food and shelter for the night."

"I shall gladly grant your plea," said the count, "for my wife has much need of someone to care for our son and educate him. Might you be interested in the employment?"

"I would be honored to work for someone so good and noble," said Beatriz.

They stepped over the guards, and the count reassured her that they would awake in an hour or two. Beatriz imagined the emperor's wrath if they returned to Rome to tell him what had happened. It seemed unlikely Antoninus would hear from these guards ever again.

The thought of her beloved husband being so quick to disbelieve her and sending her to a fate he must've known would be worse than death took her breath away. Count Magnus lifted Beatriz onto his own horse and mounted behind her, perhaps too kindly leaving the guards all three horses they'd come to the forest with.

She must leave all that behind, as well. Facing forward, she found her voice. "Why were you in the forest at this time, my lord?"

"I was going to Rome to find our son a nanny and tutor. You've saved me a fair portion of the journey."

"St. Mary has saved us both, my lord."

"She works wonders. Our house is devoted to her, as you seem to be."

Beatriz relaxed in the saddle with the certainty that no harm could come to her with such a family. They chatted about the count's household and Beatriz's experience with children. She told him she had raised and educated the emperor's son and daughter, which was far from a lie, and made her story credible with details about the palace and the prince and princess only an insider would know. She wept thinking of her dear children, now being tutored in Germany and France, and the palace she had left only hours earlier, but the count didn't see her tears.

The count's palace revealed itself between the trees, a miniature castle with crenellations and turrets, but no moat or drawbridge. It displayed the count's wealth, but apparently, he had no concern about enemies who might attack. The empress imagined sleeping inside those walls, safe from harm. "What a beautiful home," she murmured.

The count dismounted, and footmen hurried from the outbuildings to see to his horse. One of them helped Beatriz down, and she smoothed her skirts and looked up to see the count embracing a woman who must be the countess. Beatriz's own gowns were no more tasteful than the countess's. Her sleeves were embroidered with gold thread and tiny pearls, and several jeweled necklaces framed her elegant neck.

"Back so soon, husband?" she said. She looked Beatriz top to bottom. "Have you found Evander's tutor already? Where did you find someone so beautiful?"

"Flavia, this woman is well qualified to rear our son, for she can read and appears to possess no bad qualities. I believe she will be loyal to us."

Beatriz curtsied before her new mistress. "May I meet the child, my lady?"

"Of course," said the countess. "You do seem to be a very good lady." She took Beatriz's hand, and abandoning the count, the women entered the palace and crossed the courtyard, which was crowded with people busy at every imaginable task from the imperial palace, though on a smaller scale. They climbed the stairs to the top of the largest tower.

"I keep him here because it's the safest place in the palace," said the countess at the door. She let Beatriz catch her breath, then opened the door to reveal a chamber with an adult bed and a crib and pillows in every color covering everything. A young woman at the window buttoned up her blouse after breastfeeding. Only the child's head appeared outside the swaddling.

"Oh, he's tiny!" exclaimed Beatriz.

"He's four weeks," said the countess, taking him from the wet nurse, "but he's strong. We're very hopeful. He had a brother and a sister before this, but they didn't…"

"I'm so sorry for your misfortune," said Beatriz. She hadn't known that sorrow, at least, but the countess's blinked-back tears made her feel it, too. Evander fluttered his eyelids drowsily, and she was filled with an urge to snatch him up and never let him go. "May I hold him, my lady?"

The countess laid him in Beatriz's arms, always supporting his head. Beatriz loosened the swaddling and the lad grasped at her finger to bring it to is lips. Beatriz chuckled to feel the warmth of his breath.

"Oh, countess, this boy is strong. He'll grow up and bring glory to your household. It would be my honor to care for him, and teach him to read, and tell him what I know of the world from what I saw at the palace, if you'll let me." It was only then that Beatriz remembered to look at her hostess. The baby gurgled.

Countess Flavia smiled. "I can see he's fond of you already. You may stay with us tonight, and tomorrow the count and I will decide if you should raise my boy."

Beatriz insisted on sleeping in the tower with the baby and the wet nurse, allowing for no extra fuss. The two women would share the bed right next to the baby's crib. Beatriz could only bear to hand him over when they arrived downstairs in the kitchen, where the wet nurse would look after him while Beatriz dined as one more of the count and countess's guests. Suddenly weak with hunger, Beatriz had no strength to protest being seated near the head of the table, next to the countess, where everyone would notice her.

Across from her, a handsome young man demonstrated the proper sequence of wiping one's finger on the bread, then dipping it in the sauce. Beatriz had never had to think about such etiquette before, as she had always been at the head of the table, setting rules for everyone else. She was relieved to have this silent teacher, and smiled and waved at him in thanks. The grin he flashed back made it occur to her that he must think her some sort of rube who had to be taught how to behave in society.

"Ah, Beatriz," said the count, having realized they hadn't been introduced. "This is my brother, Rufus. Rufus, Beatriz is a good lady who's going to try her hand at raising Evander."

Rufus stood and walked behind the count to take Beatriz's hand and kiss it. "Welcome to our humble home. I'm most pleased to meet you, and predict you'll be spending many years with us."

Beatriz withdrew her hand discreetly. "Thank you," she whispered, not looking into his eyes. She had made up her mind to have nothing to do with men after Felix and Antoninus had nearly caused her death. Rufus returned to his seat.

"Our boy seems to love Beatriz already," said Countess Flavia. "You should've seen how he smiled."

Beatriz didn't recall any particular change in the baby's expression, but happily received more words of praise and admiration from the count. She smiled widely at everyone else at the table, and the conversation turned to other things. The empress had just pushed away the third course, thinking how grateful she was that the count hadn't mentioned the terrifying situation he'd found her in. Surrounded by welcoming faces, it was almost as if the emperor's rejection and condemnation to the forest had never happened.

"I've heard from my vassal in Rome," said one of the noblemen farther down the table. "It seems the Christians have stabilized Acre, and the emperor has already returned."

"What wonderful news," said Count Magnus. "I shall have to travel to Rome very soon."

Beatriz's muscles tensed. Would the next gossip be about the emperor's rejection of the empress after all she'd done to keep Rome stable and prosperous for two-and-a-half years? She stood up from her chair. "I must apologize to the entire company, but it's getting late. I'm sure I must leave you and put the young heir to bed. I must learn exactly how the young heir is to be treated."

"You'll miss dessert," said Rufus. "Sweet ladies should have sweets."

"No, she's right," said Countess Flavia. "I like how seriously you take your duties. You're excused."

Beatriz knelt and kissed the countess's hand, then

hurried back to the kitchen, unable to speak lest she unleash a torrent of tears.

The wet nurse cradled the babe near the fireplace. His expression seemed vacant or perhaps drowsy, but when Beatriz took him into her arms, his little face filled with light. His eyes wide, he started to giggle, and the empress chuckled, too. She felt suddenly safe, seeing what the countess had seen. He really did like her. That affection would serve as Beatriz's salvation.

"Is it time to put him to bed?" Beatriz asked. "I'd like to keep to his schedule."

"I'm feeling rather tired myself," said the wet nurse. "I'll show you how we retire."

They ascended the stairs. The wet nurse held the candle and Beatriz the baby. They switched when they arrived in Evander's room, now also Beatriz's. She watched as the nurse burped him, made sure he was clean, then laid him in the crib in fresh swaddling. The nurse rinsed her hands with water in the basin near the changing table and threw back the covers on the side of the bed closest to the crib.

"This way I don't have to go far when he gets hungry during the night," she said.

Beatriz eyed the other side of the bed. It was

closer to the fireplace, but seemed to lack a warmth she craved.

"Will you let me sleep next to him?" she asked. "Sometimes babies cry during the night because they need something else. I'd like to be there for him."

The nurse peered up at Beatriz skeptically from the bolster.

"If he really is hungry, I'll pass him to you. You won't even have to sit up."

She grunted and rolled over to make room for the empress. Beatriz touched the boy's cheek and looked into his eyes, deep blue even in the candlelight. She caressed his soft cheeks and forehead until the lids drooped and finally squeezed shut in earnest baby slumber. Fortified by his quiet contentment, she blew out the candle and found the rumpled covers by touch.

The bed strings sagged under her until she was in almost a sitting position. Why hadn't they tightened them before bed? The nurse snored next to her, and she knew the answer would have to wait until morning.

A great drowsiness overtook her body, but her mind suddenly raced. Why had Antoninus believed Felix over his beloved wife? Had the Crusade changed him? Perhaps it had all been over the moment she'd been unable to convince him to stay. Two-and-a-half years of missing him, of working so hard to protect his empire, of keeping Felix under control, all for nothing. Less than nothing! She had been the empress that morning, sure of the love of the emperor and with hopes of seeing her daughter and son again someday. Now she slept in an uncomfortable bed next to a woman she didn't know.

And yet she had to be grateful because the alternative could've been much worse.

Tears rolled down her cheeks, though she was able to stifle her sobs. But the young master seemed to sense her anguish. He began to weep loudly.

Beatriz fetched him from the crib, laid him on her chest, and put her finger to his mouth. He didn't try to latch on, but kept screaming, so when the wet nurse turned over and put her arms out to the boy, Beatriz whispered, "No, he's not hungry. I'll calm him myself." She felt his warmth against her breast and made quiet shushing sounds, and soon both the empress and the baby were fast asleep.

III.

Three years later, Evander had been weaned and had his own little bed next to Beatriz, who made sure to tighten the strings of both every evening. The wet nurse had found other work on another estate, leaving them to their secrets. Many were the nights when he climbed in with her, complaining of monsters in the shadows. She protected him from demons, and he protected her from her memories.

After a pleasant breakfast feeding porridge to her charge with the count, countess, and Rufus, Beatriz asked Evander what he would like to do that morning. She could make anything an educational event, and he was happier when he felt he had a choice.

"Forest-forest-forest," he said, clapping his hands.

"All right," said Beatriz. She wiped some porridge off his hands with the tablecloth. "You know where we'll be if you need us," the empress said to the adults.

Evander walked around the table to receive a kiss from his father. His mother smoothed his hair as well, and his Uncle Rufus pretended to punch him in the gut. It was the only combat training he'd received so far, and he always met it with squeals of laughter. Rufus cast a knowing look at Beatriz: they two were the young heir's favorite people.

Evander loved to work his little legs and could run around in the forest all morning if Beatriz didn't watch the time to avoid crankiness later. Beatriz grasped his hand. "Tell me the name of these little leaves that grow on the forest floor."

"Sorrel!" he shrieked with delight, causing a commotion in the bushes as the smaller creatures startled and sought cover.

"Hush now," said Beatriz. "We don't want to disturb the creatures here. This is their forest, after all." Some other day, he would learn that being silent in the forest was important for hunting, too.

She led him to sit by one of the bushes and modeled the kind of calm that would make the squirrels trust them enough to come out. None deigned to show themselves, but Beatriz knew the exercise had been successful when a golden butterfly alighted on Evander's hand. He didn't even flinch, but lightly sucked in air.

"See how pretty the butterfly is," whispered Beatriz.

"Butterfly." He barely exhaled, but the skittish creature darted onto a nearby bush where they could still contemplate it.

"See the pretty black spots," whispered Beatriz. "See the way she spreads and closes her wings."

The boy clapped his hands, startling the butterfly and bringing the lesson to an end. He gazed at Beatriz, deciding whether to throw a fit, but she stood as if it had all been intentional and grasped his hand.

"Off to new adventures," she said. "Remember to be quiet so the animals won't be frightened."

"Yes, Bea," he said, but soon enough, he had picked up twigs and was running along the path, rattling all the leaves in the bushes. "Shh!" he imitated.

Beatriz knew that at that age, he couldn't keep still for long. He had a long life ahead of him. There would be time for it all.

A flick between the crowns of the trees, and even

Beatriz couldn't help but exclaim, "Look! A swift!"

The boy looked up with a gasp, and never removing his gaze from the slits of blue sky above him, ran maniacally toward Beatriz knew not what goal.

"You can't catch a swift from down here, silly," she said. "They never land until they die." She too gazed at the bird, fascinated and sympathetic to its need to keep moving.

The path was clear, free of roots and branches. He must've tripped over his own foot, or a bit of uneven ground. The fall, even from his small stature, horrified Beatriz, who thought she was witnessing him dive from frenetic joyous life into the depths of death.

When she came to him, she found his face in the dirt. "Evander! Evander!" she shrieked, clutching him to her.

He coughed and pulled away. The stick he'd been holding had left a gash from his ear to his chin, far too close to his tender neck.

Beatriz scooped him up, and he became limp as she ran back to the house. She hadn't realized they'd come so far into the forest. What had she been thinking? Tears blurred her vision, and she nearly ran into the horse that had stepped onto the path.

"Beatriz, what happened?" asked Rufus.

"He fell," she choked. She lifted Evander so he could see.

After a moment frozen with dismay, Rufus took the boy into his arms. "Get on. I'll take you both back and send for a physician."

"No, I'll only slow you down," said Beatriz. She wanted some time to reflect on what had happened. "I'll follow on foot."

Rufus stared at her with concern while the horse tried to respond to his awkward commands, and then they sped off. Beatriz collapsed on the twig-covered earth and wept until she felt her heart was empty. Evander had become everything to the empress, the reason she could keep living when everyone in Rome thought she was dead and the way she forgot about her former life. Without him, where could she turn?

Her self-pity sated, she stood, dusted off her knees, and hurried down the twisting path to the chapel in the building near the stable. She saw the groom tending to Rufus's horse, which renewed her hope. She swung the chapel door open and knelt before the image of St. Mary.

"You, Blessed Virgin Mother, who didn't see fit to spare me the infamy and lies of my husband, but who did save my life and grant me a humble new one, save innocent Evander now. He's like a son to me, and I know you wouldn't want to see me suffer as you did for your Son. In saving him, you save me, too, for if this little boy dies, I fear I will fall into desperation. Let me serve you in raising Evander well. I won't disappoint you if you save him now."

"Beatriz."

The empress was jarred out of her prayer. Through her tears, she saw Rufus standing in the doorway. "Is Evander all right?"

"They've put him in his mother's bed, and they think a physician can come from the town within the hour."

"I'll go to him. He must be frightened."

Beatriz headed for the door, wiping her cheeks on her sleeve. Rufus caught her by the elbow, and she scanned his face in confusion.

"The first time I saw you, I was captivated by your beauty." His breathing was ragged. "For these three years, I've waited for you to look my way, but your only thought is for Evander. But think about it. We're his two favorite people. We're meant to be together, for his sake. Today demonstrates that we don't know what's going to happen tomorrow. Let's live today."

He let go of her sleeve, and Beatriz thought she

might get away, but too quickly, he forced her face toward his. The kiss was greedy and had so much pull that Beatriz thought he might tear her lips off. She beat on Rufus's chest, and when he paused for breath, she took advantage and wrenched herself free.

"How dare you?" she shrieked, backing away. "Here in the church, with Evander on the brink of death. I haven't looked at you in three years because I'm never going to."

She picked up her hem and rushed past some of the stable boys, who must've seen the whole exchange. The countess slept in a bower off the great hall. It made sense that they would take Evander to that room, avoiding the tower stairs. Many servants clustered about the door, but when they saw Beatriz, they made way for her.

Countess Flavia knelt at the bed, where Evander was barely visible under a multitude of blankets. She ran her hands through his sweaty hair while he struggled against the count and two body servants, who maintained pressure on the boy's arms and legs.

"Beatriz," said the countess. "He's been asking for you."

"Bea," the boy said, not opening his mouth too wide. "They're being mean to me."

The countess stood at her side, and the empress knelt near the boy. He visibly relaxed.

"I think you can let go now," Beatriz told the count and servants.

"We're waiting for the physician, but maybe you learned some physical medicine at the palace?" the countess commented.

"The imperial palace had a resident physician, so I wasn't called on to know much," Beatriz murmured. She stroked the good side of Evander's face. "They were just trying to keep you still," she told the boy. "You must keep very still now, and breathe calmly, and it will hurt less, I promise."

There was blood on the bolster, which concerned her, but with the boy calm, Beatriz was able to see the cut. It was long, but not deep.

"You're going to get all better very soon," she told Evander with some conviction. She looked up at the body servants. "We need to wash this with gentle soap and apply a linen bandage. Then when the physician comes, he'll decide if he needs to apply leeches."

"Don't let that woman near the boy!" Rufus's voice rang out from the doorway.

Beatriz stood, and Evander started to thrash and cry again.

Rufus strode to the countess. "I saw it all. She did this on purpose. She's trying to kill or cripple the boy and leave you without an heir."

"Beatriz? That's not possible." Countess Flavia backed away from her brother-in-law and looked to her husband. "She's been with us for three years, and I think she would rather die than see Evander come to harm."

"It's true," said Beatriz. "Rufus wasn't there. He didn't see Evander trip on something in the path. Who could ever imagine I would harm Evander?"

Count Magnus took his brother by the shoulders. "I know you're upset, but there's no need to blame anyone. Evander's going to be fine."

"He is?" Rufus looked at the boy for the first time. Passing by Beatriz uncomfortably close, he knelt at the bedside. Patting Evander's hair, he received the boy's frankly loving gaze. Rufus kissed his forehead and turned to the count. "His first battle scar. Everyone will be afraid when they see him."

Beatriz stayed across the room from Rufus while they waited for the physician, and though he seemed to take no notice of her, she caught him glowering more than once. Evander remained calm for the examination only because Beatriz held his little hand, and he squeezed as he needed to. All his fear was compressed into a clasp that felt feather-light to the empress. It seemed the whole estate watched the proceedings, and a collective sigh reverberated around the room and into the great hall when the physician pronounced the young heir out of danger.

"The Blessed Mother has answered my prayers," Beatriz told the countess, "and yours, too, I think."

The physician gave Beatriz a vial of salve to apply twice a day, and praised the way she'd cleaned and dressed the wound. Seeing the professional appraisal of the empress's work, Countess Flavia declared that Beatriz should sleep in that bed with the young heir and make sure he didn't pick off his bandage during the night. So, after a long day of keeping Evander distracted from his prescribed bed rest with stories and games and soup ladled into his mouth, pursed against moving the wounded area too much, Beatriz settled in next to her charge as usual, though in an unusual setting.

They brought a small table to the bedside so the salve, linens, and clean water were always near. His parents kissed Evander good night, and though Rufus was nowhere to be seen, Beatriz didn't miss him. The count and countess shut the door, but a sort of celebration in the great hall meant Beatriz had to hold Evander close to her, whispering and singing.

Even so, he fretted over his wound and asked for his own bed long into the night, after the festivity was over.

"If you stay still now and get lots of rest, maybe tomorrow they'll let us play outside a little. I know it's hard to sleep in a strange bed, but maybe we'll return to our room in the tower tomorrow. Even if that cut leaves a scar, you'll only be more handsome. Any woman who sees you will never forget you, and any man will take care to be your friend. You can tell everyone the dragon got in one good swipe before you slew him."

Beatriz felt tremendous relief talking about Evander's future, even as she veered into delirium. When he finally settled down, Beatriz fell into the deep sleep of exhaustion.

IV.

Beatriz woke when she felt something smooth pressed into her palm. In the minimal morning light streaming from the shuttered window, she saw a dark, hunched form glide to the door and slip away. The object in her hand was a knife with a horn handle.

Beatriz flung the knife across the room. "Evander, Evander, dear." He didn't respond to her whispers. She touched his shoulder to wake him, and his shirt was soaked.

A sense that her world was coming to its end made Beatriz embrace the boy as if nothing were wrong. But the little body that she'd cared for and kept safe from harm for three years as her own son was lifeless.

Her eyes adjusted to the light. The bandage was undisturbed, but just beneath it, in an appalling mockery of her healing skills, his white neck was cut through with a red channel. It didn't seem real. It seemed like one of those awful paintings of martyrs that evoked pity and devotion.

Shaking, Beatriz crossed the room along the same path of the earlier hunched form and opened the door to find several servants preparing the table for breakfast in the resplendent light from the open windows of the great hall. Before she said anything, everyone stopped what they were doing to stare at her, and she realized the entire front of her nightdress was bright red. It didn't seem possible such a small boy could have so much blood in him.

"Fetch the count and countess," Beatriz managed. She slid down the wall to avoid fainting and wept into her hands. She didn't look up when she felt one of the servants walk past her to peer inside the room.

The servant screamed, then shook the empress. "What happened? Beatriz, what happened?"

She refused to remove her hands from her face, but finally stood and backed away when the servant said, "No, countess, don't look. Count Magnus, keep her away from her room!"

The uproar was ceaseless as more members of the

household ran into the great hall, but Beatriz ignored it all, consumed by the pain she saw in the count and countess as they wept into each other's tunics at the foot of the bed. The count had found the knife that had killed his son on the floor and held it limply, as if he couldn't understand what it was.

"She killed him to disgrace us!" roared Rufus from the other end of the hall.

"Of course I didn't!" said Beatriz. She supported herself on the great table.

"Didn't I tell you yesterday she wished Evander ill? Now it's too late!" Rufus ran across the hall, knocking servants out of his way, and grabbed Beatriz. "I shall take vengeance upon you for his death."

Beatriz screamed impotently. "I would never harm Evander, and you know it." Struggling against Rufus, she caught the countess's eye. "It was him. He did it!"

Countess Flavia threw her hands up in shock, and Rufus turned to the table. Beatriz ran back toward the countess's room. He caught her at the door and beat her with a metal trencher. She fell to the floor and tried to deflect the blows with her arms. He pressed the edge against her neck. It wasn't sharp, but it took her breath away. She pushed against Rufus's sinewy arms to relieve the pressure.

But then she thought it would be just as well to die and let the scoundrel have his lies. Without Evander, Beatriz didn't know what to keep living for. She closed her eyes and lay still.

Suddenly, involuntarily, the empress gasped, taking in air. The thin, cold edge of the trencher no longer threatened her life. Her eyes opened, and she saw Rufus held between two of the count's men. But it was the countess who seized the trencher and tossed it back on the table.

"I don't know what to believe," said Countess Flavia. "But we can't have the count's brother meting out justice in the family palace."

"If she killed him, she must be taken out and burned," said one of the servants. He was newer, and hadn't witnessed the years Beatriz had cared for Evander.

Beatriz shook her head. She wanted to take the chance to tell everyone what she'd seen, that the crouched form must've been Rufus, but she could only cough.

"She should be beheaded, as she practically beheaded the young heir," said another servant, who'd looked inside the room.

"No, no," said the countess.

"Let me take her to the port," said Rufus. "If we send her out to sea, her fate will be in God's hands."

Count Magnus stood between Rufus and the countess, cupping the knife in his hands. "I think this is the solution. It's hard to believe Beatriz did this, but my boy is dead. No one else could've done it, and someone must pay. Does anyone disagree?"

In the silence that followed, Beatriz found her feet, coughing, only to be seized by the same guards who'd kept Rufus from killing her.

"Come along then, to the port," said Rufus, waving the guards to the door.

"Not so fast," said the countess. She approached the empress and looked into her eyes. "Beatriz, I don't know who committed this crime, but it's best for you to leave us now, to our grief."

Beatriz struggled to speak. The countess's long relationship with her and her gentility when everyone else was turning barbaric were the empress's last desperate hope. Seeing her struggle, the countess took a wine jug still on the table from the previous night's celebration and held the spout to Beatriz's lips.

They were only dregs, but Beatriz gulped all she could. The guards started escorting her to the hall's exit even as she coughed and twisted, trying to talk to the countess. Near the door, she wheezed, "Wait! It was Rufus. I saw him!" She hardly felt the blow that knocked her unconscious.

V.

Beatriz awoke with a gasp in a space darkened by damask curtains. She sat up and felt fresh clothes on her body, and her hair was tied back from her face. The countess must've done those favors to her dignity, but Beatriz preferred not to think about who else might've seen her unresponsive body being cleaned and dressed.

She wondered what had become of the blood-soaked nightdress, and the whole terrifying morning crashed down on her. If she'd let Rufus have his way with her, he wouldn't have killed poor, innocent Evander. Would a sinful union have been so bad if it meant watching Evander grow into a much better man than his uncle? No, sharing a bed might've been enough for a time, but then Rufus would've made more demands impossible to satisfy. Beatriz couldn't accede to any man's desires, anyway, since she was still married to the emperor. Even though he thought she was dead, her vow to him had been for her whole life.

The changing light and the sounds of hooves and wheels on a stone road told her at least her dizziness wasn't entirely due to the lump on her head. She felt it painfully under her hair against the side of the carriage every time it lurched. If she'd eaten anything at all the night before, she was sure she'd be heaving it out on the side of the road.

Instinctively, she reached for the curtains to part them, but her hand was stopped. Each wrist was tied to a different metal ring on the carriage wall. She couldn't reach her ankles to loosen the binding that held them together, either. She tugged, but the rings were sturdy. She wondered if this was a special carriage for criminals.

"I'm not a delinquent! I've committed no crime!" Her voice disappeared in the noise of the road, but she thought it was stronger than before.

The carriage rumbled on for another hour. Beatriz's joints ached, and she needed some cool, clean water to replenish her tears for Evander and for her life as the Empress of Rome, which seemed so long ago it might as well never have happened. She often thought she would give anything for the jolting to stop, and finally it did, with a last few chaotic thumps and bangs.

She couldn't suppress a sigh of impatience when nothing seemed to happen. Men murmured near the curtain, but she couldn't make out what they said, because she also heard the clamor of fishermen moving equipment, sailors shouting orders, and fishmongers marketing their wares. The smell of the sea wafted through the curtain fabric.

This was the same port where the empress had last hugged her daughter when she left for France, where her young son had given her a salute, trying to look like a man ready to take on the world before heading to his education in Germany. It was also where Antoninus had departed for the crusade that turned him against her. She hadn't seen him off because she had been responsible for Rome in his absence. She wondered if that far-off place had influenced his attitude toward her, or perhaps the sea itself had changed him.

The curtains finally parted, and silhouetted against the sky full of gulls and terns was the man she'd been expecting, Rufus. She was ready.

"Evander—your nephew, whom you always said

you loved more than yourself—you killed him just to have your revenge on me. Why didn't you just kill me and have done with it?"

"If you don't shut up, I'll have to gag you," Rufus muttered, reaching for the rings where her ropes were hooked in.

Beatriz bit her lip. She would save her words for when they would have effect. He didn't look up at her, but bound her wrists together in front, then untied her ankles. He wound the other end of her wrist bindings around his left hand and jumped down from the carriage, dragging Beatriz with him.

She collapsed on the filthy dock.

Rufus tugged on the rope. "Get up. You can't look mussed if we're going to get a good price for you."

"What?"

"Hush! I want them to see your pretty face, but if you force me, I'll put a bag over your head."

Beatriz was dragged along so Rufus could talk to Roman fishermen and sailors. He told the men, who looked like honest hard workers to Beatriz, that she was a witch and that he didn't care what else they did with her, but they should take her out to sea and drown her afterward. He expected to earn some coin for granting this privilege. Whenever Rufus looked away from her, Beatriz shook her head vigorously and mouthed to the others that it was all lies. No one, it seemed, wanted to become involved in whatever was happening between Beatriz and Rufus.

But then Rufus pulled her toward a group of seven sailors wearing turbans. "These will pay me and won't ask questions," said Rufus, before he launched into a greeting and fast-paced conversation with them.

He knew their language from his time in the East. Although Beatriz held her bound wrists to her heart in what she hoped looked to them like pleading for mercy and shook her head with all her might, one of the sailors handed a purse that seemed to be full of coins to Rufus.

He opened it, and a golden gleam reflected off the coins and made cadaverous hollows of his eyes. He chuckled at Beatriz. "I've told them to drown you, but they seem to want to take you to Syria and sell you into a sultan's harem. Good luck."

Rufus handed Beatriz's rope to the sailor closest to him and ambled back to the carriage on the other side of the port, looking back at Beatriz and fingering the coins in the purse with a leer.

Beatriz screamed. At first it was wordless with terror, then she shouted "No!" in protest at being pulled along the dock and gangway and onto the deck of their ship. Other sailors throughout the port looked up, but they'd all spoken with Rufus by then, so her enslavement must've seemed an inevitable outcome, and no one came to her aid.

"Quiet now," barked one of the sailors, who had more jewels in his turban than the others. Beatriz thought he must be the captain.

"My name is Beatriz, Empress of Rome. I will not be silent!"

All the sailors had come aboard, and they looked on her with pity. The captain said something in his language, and one of the bigger sailors picked Beatriz up as if she were a doll, draped her over his shoulder, and carried her down the ladder into the hold.

The ship's interior was dark, but in the light coming through a couple of portholes, Beatriz could see that the hold was nearly empty. They must've sold all their goods from the East and been headed home to enjoy their earnings or load more to sell. The sailor left her sitting next to a barrel without bothering to try and communicate, and she realized she must be the prize merchandise for their return trip.

According to Rufus, she was to be sold into slavery to a sultan, though he'd told them to drown her. She wasn't sure which destiny was worse, or whether there was any good reason to draw breath anymore. She drew her knees up and laid her forehead on them, shaking. Her despair had surpassed useless tears.

By the time the ship had lurched out of the dock, Beatriz lay prone on the hard, dusty slats in a state between sleeping and waking. Where was her bed with the tightened strings and the gentle boy to care for? Gone forever.

She closed her eyes against further atrocities when she heard someone coming down the ladder. He nudged Beatriz's shoulder, and she opened her eyes to behold the captain.

"We're at sea now. You can move about ship," he said. He untied her bindings with an ease that made Beatriz feel incompetent. He stood at the bottom of the ladder, motioning to her. "Come."

She felt free without the bindings, but couldn't find the strength to move. "I don't think I can make it above decks," she whispered. "I need water and food."

The captain's gaze darted around the hold. He strode to one of the barrels. "We're taking wine back for Christians in Syria."

It did look like a wine barrel. The captain went through a door at the far end of the hold and came back out with a bowl. He held it under the barrel's tap and filled it halfway. He was so steady on his feet that Beatriz didn't notice the way the ship rocked back and forth until she sat up to receive the bowl. She tried to drink moderately, but her body was starving for the sustenance the bowl offered, and sure enough, a purple stain appeared on the front of her apron.

"That's our merchandise. I can't let you have much more. Can you climb the ladder now?" The captain held out his hand to Beatriz, and she accepted it and pulled herself up.

The captain ascended the ladder with the swiftness of someone who had done it all his life. Beatriz felt almost as limp as poor Evander had been in the bed next to her. She followed the captain slowly, holding her skirts with one hand, and making sure the other hand had a good grip before making a move.

She emerged into a bright world of endless blue sky and a brisk breeze. She gingerly set her feet on deck and observed the sailors, who followed the captain's orders efficiently. She looked over the side and was hypnotized by the rush of water as the ship skimmed along.

The wind whipped her hair against her neck, and

a feeling of unstoppable progress overcame her.

But progress to where? With one last effort, she could climb over the side and drown all her sorrows in the sea. It was what some people wanted, anyway.

The captain stood next to her and motioned to the horizon. "The coast is there, but it's too far to swim, so I was able to untie you. Come." He helped her stumble across the deck and opened the door to a large, relatively comfortable room. "This is my accommodation, but you can stay here, at least until you're stronger. Sit. I'll have food brought."

Beatriz sat at a wide desk that was obviously meant for poring over maps and looked out the large window. Being treated humanely agreed with her, and after she ate the surprisingly tasty bean stew another sailor had set in front of her, other ways forward began to form in her mind.

If she could continue to interact pleasantly with the captain, and find ways to get on the sailors' good side—cleaning, washing up the dishes, or braiding ropes were all she could think of just then—perhaps she could convince them not to sell her to a sultan. She couldn't go back to being an empress, she knew, and it would be too painful to try to tutor another child so soon after losing Evander. But if there were Christians in Syria who bought wine from these sailors, perhaps there was a community of devotees who would let her join them. It would have to be a mendicant order, she realized, since she had only the wine-stained clothes she wore. But it would be a quiet life, devoted to the Mother of God, away from men.

This new possibility, the empress's exhaustion, and the steady, gentle rocking of the captain's berth plunged her into a deep sleep.

She woke only when she was thrown from the berth against the desk and to the floor. She held onto the bolted table leg against the violent movements of the cabin, in her grogginess unsure what terrifying place she was in. The floor seemed to rise to a great height, then dropped again, and Beatriz realized they must've become caught in a storm. Another wave like that, and the ship wouldn't stay upright.

She crawled back across the accommodation to the berth on hands full of splinters. The shutters on the window had broken loose and scattered all over. Perhaps the chair had already been lost through the window, for it was nowhere to be found. Water sputtered onto the desk haphazardly. Beatriz felt glad she had no possessions to lose out the window, and briefly wondered whether it would be better to float out to sea herself.

She sat on the berth and gripped the ledge for hours. She lost the bean stew she'd eaten, and it was washed away just as quickly. The accommodation door flew open at one point, and Beatriz watched as some of the sailors lashed down equipment and kept each other from falling overboard under a cloud-darkened sky. They were shouting, but she couldn't hear anything over the thundering water.

She didn't let go of the ledge even when they seemed to have regained control of the ship. The day dawned bright, and some hope entered her heart, but she maintained her grim hold on the berth ledge when she felt the gentle bump of docking and heard the cries of gulls and fishmongers.

The captain stood in the accommodation doorway. "Are you all right?"

"Yes. I've been tossed about, but I don't think I'm injured. Did all the sailors make it?" Beatriz said, finally releasing the berth.

"We have several injuries. We're stopping at Syracuse. We must find a physician and mend the damage to the ship."

"I can help with the repairs." Beatriz remembered her plan to get into their good graces.

"I'm sorry," he replied, holding out a rope. "I can't let you run away."

"But I have nowhere to go," she said, knowing she would try to escape, anyway.

The captain took her hands in his to tie her wrists. "Oh, look at that!"

"Splinters," said Beatriz. "They're painful."

"I'll see if I can find a remedy in the town. But for now, I must bind you." He tied sinuous sailor's knots around her wrists, then led the cord to her ankles, which he also bound, leaving just enough slack for her to stand.

She could hop across the cabin, but she dared not appear on deck for fear they would think she was trying something. And so, she spent their five days in port almost by herself. Every time she thought of poor little Evander, she tried to cheer herself up with thoughts of her daughter and son. But Antoninus had probably written them lies about her. What must they imagine about their mother now?

Two able-bodied sailors came the second day to mount new shutters in the window. The captain brought her one large meal every day and sat on the new chair to keep her company while she dined on the berth as well as she could with her hands still bound. He cured her splinters with warm water and salve, and patiently picked out the last stubborn spikes with a needle.

He was a pleasant conversationalist, and with each day, Beatriz felt more hopeful that he would remember her humanity and think twice about selling her into slavery. She longed to ask him to bring her a book to read, or any other amusement, but knew that the sailors would be more likely to set her free later if she made no demands now.

"The winds bode favorably tomorrow, and the ship is better now than when we left Ostia. We leave tomorrow morning," the captain said on the fifth day.

Beatriz looked forward to going out to sea solely in order to be released from the ropes. Her wrists chafed no matter what position she put them in, and it was sometimes hard to avoid her legs falling asleep. "I suppose that means you won't have time to accompany me while I dine anymore."

"No." He sighed, and the empress hoped it meant he'd enjoyed their strange time together.

"I'll miss our conversations," she said.

He took her hands in his. "So will I."

He left the accommodation, and Beatriz's heart was in her throat. She tried to remember the sneering faces of Felix and Rufus. Did the captain look like them? He seemed so much gentler, so much more civilized than she'd expected. She reminded herself that he hadn't tried anything yet. He'd left the cabin courteously, and wouldn't have an opportunity for anything else before they arrived.

"St. Mary, protect me," she murmured to herself. Still, she couldn't rest that night. She only drifted off in the early hours of the morning, comforted by the now-familiar sounds of the captain barking orders and the soldiers trimming or unfolding sails. They were competent seamen.

Beatriz woke when the ship lurched and skidded sideways, then abruptly turned and urged forward. She didn't feel the action of waves, and the movement wasn't the natural undulation of the previous days of the voyage.

She stumbled to the window and wrenched open one of the shutters with her bound hands. The sky was empty, with no clouds and no birds. The sea moved as much as a polished glass mirror, and yet the bow sliced through it, carrying them more swiftly than ever before. The light splashing of the ship's wake in the calm only increased the eeriness.

She sat at the desk and watched the unchanging world slide by, smoother than if she were watching from a carriage.

She became aware of the crew's shouts, but they soon quieted. Perhaps they, too, understood that there was nothing they could do to stop whatever was happening.

At last, the captain came into the room and knelt to untie Beatriz's ankles. "We're becalmed, and yet the ship is moving. It's off course, and we can't do anything to correct it."

"I haven't done much sailing, but even I know this isn't the way a ship normally moves," she replied. Perhaps their shared bewilderment could be her way into making the sailors consider her more than cargo.

He freed her wrists. "The men are saying you make bad luck. That we'll never return to Syria with you aboard."

"Of course it's not true," said Beatriz, massaging her ankles to loosen up the cramps. It seemed no one ever did anything but lie about her.

"They want to throw you overboard."

"Right now?" The calm outside the window made it seem like they were on a lagoon in the mountains with plenty of villages nearby. But they were in the middle of the Mediterranean with no land in sight. Beatriz knew the unforgiving sea would drag her under before she could cry for help. "They can't! You can't let them!" She latched onto the captain's arm, pleading.

"I don't want them to. I like you very much."

He put his arms around her brusquely, and she was reminded of too many other moments in her life after the emperor left on crusade. She pushed away, but he confirmed her fears by holding her tighter.

"If you become my lover," he whispered in her ear, "I can protect you. The men will not harm you, and when we come to Syria, I will give you a house with servants. I won't sell you to the sultan, but treat you well for the rest of your life. After you convert to Islam."

"I can't do that," said Beatriz. "I can't do any of that." She struggled against his arms, but he had hers pinned to her sides.

"You must. You have no choice. You must become mine or the sailors will leave your beauty on the bottom of the sea."

Even this man, who had seemed so gentle with her, could only see her as a slave, whether to sell or for his personal use. She had never felt so alone.

Then her despair turned to righteous rage. What right did anyone have to treat her this way? If she had forgotten that the Queen of Heaven always defended her, it was only because that Celestial Lady had abandoned her.

Beatriz gazed at the roof of the cabin, imagining Heaven beyond it. "St. Mary, you have no pity for me, nor does your Son remember me. What am I to do?" She stopped struggling and went limp against the captain. "Blessed Virgin, I'm in your hands."

Take your hands off her. If you don't, you'll perish right now.

The captain released Beatriz to throw his hands up in surprise. "Who said that?"

The voice had been feminine, and rang out so clear and authoritative, it could only have been St. Mary. Beatriz opened the cabin door to see all the sailors on deck, pointing at the sky and variously cowering or running in circles. When the captain emerged from the accommodation, the sailors shouted at him in their language. He made signs of assent and went to Beatriz where she waited near the side.

"They're saying it does not please God to use you for our pleasure."

"That much is true," said Beatriz.

The ship came to a stop. Beatriz looked, and it was as if they'd docked and put out a gangplank. The piece of land was hardly even an island, just a rock with some scrub sprouting at the top, but it was level with the ship's side, and it seemed as if Beatriz was meant to step up and stay there.

The sailors shouted and made gestures that she should do exactly that.

She imagined standing on that rock, alone, with nothing to see for miles around, only unyielding sunlight beating down on her. The cabin suddenly looked like a refuge. But the sternness in the captain's eyes let her know that his proposal for her to become a renegade and break her vow to the emperor was no longer on offer. She felt like a fox about to leap off a cliff, a hunting party on her tail. She didn't feel it in her to climb the side and reach the rock.

The empress put her hands up in surrender.

VI.

One of the larger sailors snatched Beatriz up, threw her over his shoulder, and climbed the side. He dropped her unceremoniously on the bracken and was back on deck before she could protest.

Beatriz sat up and squinted down into the eyes of the captain, whose countenance was stony. The sun felt relentlessly hot on her skin, and she wondered how long they would remain like that. With the ship becalmed, the sailors would die of thirst or starvation right along with the empress. It depended on the Blessed Virgin's wishes for them.

A breeze strong enough to stir the hem of her skirts brushed past Beatriz's face. The sailors on deck murmured to each other, and the captain's gaze on Beatriz faltered. Another gust rattled the mainsail.

The captain shouted orders as the wind picked up. With the sails unfurled, the ship slid smoothly away from the rock. The empress crouched under the pressure of the wind and kept her gaze on the ship, the only visible thing on the water, until it dipped beyond the horizon. The sky had become covered with black clouds, and waves crashed all around the rock, engulfing Beatriz's feet.

Beatriz stood with her hands out and faced the wind, daring it to knock her into the water. A scream had been building inside her for years, since the moment Felix had laid his hands on her. It had gained power when Antoninus sent her to die without a second thought, when she lost the chance to see her children ever again, when Rufus embraced her, and especially when that miscreant robbed the world of little Evander. It stood back when the captain treated her humanely, and she hoped for a simple life in the East. But now that every person she'd ever cared for, every possibility for peace she'd ever come upon, and every hope she'd ever held to had been mercilessly taken from her, the scream pressed on her heart and clawed at her throat.

She loosed it to the winds. No one heard it but St. Mary.

Without knowing how, she'd fallen onto the

brambles. Thorns pierced her skin and added to her weeping.

"Oh, Blessed Virgin," she whispered as a wave crashed over her head, soaking her with its freezing needles. "Am I to meet my end now, after so many trials, because yet again I wouldn't satisfy men's primitive instincts? If it is to be so, let me go to you quickly. Do not let me languish here, far from hope, far from you."

As the next wave crushed her against the rock, a beam of white light seared the sky. It lasted much longer than lightning, and the longer Beatriz contemplated it, the less pain she felt in her body, the less the sea whipped at the rock. The empress opened her mouth, and found that she felt no thirst even after having screamed with all her might. A satisfaction settled about her, as if she never needed to eat again.

The beam of light transformed gently into St. Mary. The Queen of Heaven wore velvet and silk and a crown that gleamed with jewels in every color, but her face was simple, much like that of Beatriz's mother. It was the most beautiful face in the world. She nodded at Beatriz.

"Empress, you have never been faint of heart," said the Mother of God. A delicate green sprig with small white flowers appeared in her cupped hand. "Accept this herb, which has great virtue for curing the illness of those who are untouchable. Now is the time to redeem others with your unfailing goodness."

Too astounded to act, Beatriz let St. Mary tuck the plant behind her ear. The empress awoke without ever having known she'd been asleep.

Her body maintained its sense of wholeness and lack of need. She lazily stretched her arms, looking at a blue sky with fluffy white clouds. When she lifted her head, the sprig with white flowers was under it. She clasped it in her hands.

"Mother of God, blessed are those who trust in you, for they will never lack your great mercy as long as they obey and offer thanks to you."

On the horizon, a ship approached. When it came close enough, Beatriz began to wave her arms. Two men in Christian clothes took a boat and rowed to the rock.

"Hello there," Beatriz shouted down to them. "Where are you headed?"

"We're a group of humble pilgrims, men and women, headed to Jerusalem."

Beatriz tucked the herb into the pocket in her apron. "I'm a pilgrim, too. Won't you take me with you?"

They helped her climb down into the rowboat. Their touch on her hips and ankles was chaste, and Beatriz felt so elated, she wanted to sing. Instead, she steadied herself on the bench while they pushed off and said, "Thank you. I don't know what I would've done if St. Mary hadn't sent you."

"Truly you should thank St. Mary and not us," said one pilgrim as he rowed. "We were blown a little off course and would never have found you if we'd been able to continue as we'd planned."

"Well, this calls for a hymn to the Blessed Virgin," said Beatriz.

"We like Ave Maris Stella while we sail," said the other pilgrim. "We have many different voices aboard, so the sound is full."

Once they'd all climbed aboard the ship, two other pilgrims secured the rowboat while men and women of every station came on deck to greet Beatriz with hand clasps and embraces.

"My name is Beatriz. Thank you for rescuing me. I hear you sing a wonderful Ave Maris Stella. Shall we?"

"Aren't you tired?" asked one of the women. "How long have you been stranded? May we offer you some food or wine?"

"I have nothing in my heart but rejoicing," said

Beatriz, and her smile convinced them. Thus, with singing and goodwill, in five days she and the twelve pilgrims arrived in Gythion to replenish their stores.

Beatriz was helping some of the pilgrims organize barrels and boxes belowdecks, but she heard the voices of the captain and someone who must be from Gythion. The empress climbed the ladder and found that there were in fact many men from the port on deck, and they gazed sternly at the pilgrims.

"You might as well stay below," one of the men told her. "They aren't letting us disembark. In fact, it seems they want us to leave the dock."

Remembering her successful diplomatic talks during the years the emperor was away, Beatriz strode toward the Gythionite who seemed to be in charge. The whitewashed city behind him seemed peaceful enough under the blue sky.

"What's the problem?" she asked. "Why aren't we welcome here?"

He blinked with surprise. "You aren't the problem," he replied, responding to Beatriz's authority with a slight bow. "It's for your safety. There's a leper in the port, waiting to be taken to a colony, and we don't want to spread the infection to anyone from abroad."

"He's untouchable? Take me to him," said Beatriz in a way that left no room for protest.

"We can't let you off the boat," the man insisted.

"All I need is a chalice or cup and a little clean water, and that poor man will no longer need to be banished."

Beatriz pulled the plant from her apron pocket. It looked as fresh as it had in the dream, and the sun's rays made the tiny white flowers glisten like dewdrops. The man threw his hands up in surprise. He seemed convinced as he started shouting at his companions in Greek, and they made way for Beatriz, flanking the gangplank onto the dock.

She nodded at each man of Gythion as she stepped onto the dock, and her pilgrim companions followed her. The Gythionite leader took her by the arm, saying, "Allow me."

Beatriz and the twelve pilgrims, guided by the gruff men who appeared to be judges, attracted many stares throughout the port. By the time they arrived at the hospital, most of the townspeople had joined the impromptu procession. Murmurs of hesitation sounded through the crowd when they saw where Beatriz was headed.

The building looked enough like a place for people to stay, and to be cured if they were ill, with a large open area at the front door and many windows on the second floor that could reflect many rooms or one large dormitory with many beds. But there was none of the bustle of a port hospital, none of the comings and goings. In fact, there seemed to be no one at all.

"Are you sure this is the hospital?" asked Beatriz.

"When the leper arrived, no one else dared to stay. Only the priest has stopped by to take his confession before he travels. He must be here somewhere, taking care of himself," said the leader.

"Ea," called Beatriz, nearing the back of the building. "Anyone there?"

In a doorway at the back appeared a ghostly form, silhouetted against the light from the windows behind it.

"No one but a leper. Are you here to take me to the island?" He leaned forward on a walking stick and blinked at Beatriz. Even from where she stood, she could see that his face was covered in red blotches. "You're not the type I was expecting."

Beatriz paused, turning the plant in her hand and contemplating the power it gave her. "I'm not here to take you away. I'm here to cure you."

The man progressed toward her, step by unsure step, tapping the cane against the hardened earth. He wasn't wrapped up in linen the way Beatriz had expected, but wore a tunic in the style of the Peloponnesus, like all the other residents of Gythion. The sores that obscured the features on his face and neck looked like burns, but on his tanned hands, the blotches were lighter in color, with the look of alabaster. Beatriz balked as he drew near as if to take the plant. The leader stepped between them.

"It doesn't hurt," the leper said. "Thank you for your concern."

"I'm glad you aren't suffering," said Beatriz.

"Oh, I never said that," replied the man, lifting his cane. "I had a family and a business and friends, and they've all been taken away from me. I didn't ask to be shunned by everyone I've ever known. I've never harmed anyone and I confess all my personal sins, so I don't know how or why God has cursed me with this contagion."

"That's enough," said the leader. "This good woman doesn't have to help you."

"It's all right," said Beatriz, resting her hand on the leader's to calm him. "Good sir, if you are without sin, all you have to do is trust in St. Mary and bring me some clean water to boil."

The leper looked at the plant skeptically, but brushed past Beatriz and the crowd of pilgrims and townspeople, who hurried to make way, to the hearth, where a large cookpot hung over the fire. "This is the last of the fresh water they left behind when they abandoned me here," he said, lifting a clay jug.

Beatriz joined him at the hearth. "Go ahead and pour a cup's worth into the pot." She grasped the rod to stoke the flames, and gasps of horror circled through the crowd.

"Beatriz, you mustn't touch what he's been touching," said one of her pilgrim companions.

"It's all right," she said with a smile. "The Queen of Heaven has decided I've suffered enough. This disease won't affect me."

More murmurs surged from the crowd. Perhaps they were saying she'd lost her mind. Beatriz worked the flames up to get the water boiling faster.

"And even if it did reach me, all I'd have to do is drink the tisane from this plant." She tossed the plant—stem, leaves, and flowers—into the pot and winked at the leper, who startled.

"You seem sure about this," he said.

"The time for doubt and hesitation is past. Believe me, you won't have to let anyone take you to any island. You'll be able to return to your family soon."

She turned her attention to the way the plant

floated in the water, hoping that everything she'd said was true. How could it not be? The Mother of God wouldn't say she was rewarding Beatriz's fortitude and give her a simple sprig of mint, would she?

When the water boiled, she had the leper help her take the pot off the flames and set it on the cold ashes around the hearth. She dipped a ladle into the tisane and brought it to the leper's malformed lips. He accepted and took the handle for himself so he could drink at his own pace. He didn't stop until all the tisane in the ladle was gone.

"It's delicious," he said. "Even if it does nothing to help me, people would pay for it on a cold winter evening." He chuckled, and his lips were smooth, no longer cracked and scaled. He covered his mouth with his hand in surprise.

"I can feel my face!" he yelped. "I haven't felt my face in years." The red sores on his face and neck peeled away and dropped to the earthen floor, leaving skin that looked freshly washed and shaven. He held his hands out, and the light blotches on them flaked off and joined the angry red scabs on the floor. Laughing, he shook his tunic, and more skin patches in all colors cascaded from underneath.

The man who had been leprous spun around like

a dervish. "Look at me!" he shouted. "You have no excuse to reject me now!"

He ran to Beatriz, who watched in as much amazement as everyone else, and threw his arms around her. When she reflexively backed away, he probably thought it was due to his previous disease.

"It's all right. I'm healed, just as you said." He stared at her fervently. "How can I ever thank you for giving me my life and my family back? What payment can I make?"

"I'll accept no payment but lodging at this hospital for my humble pilgrim friends and me."

"I was the hospitaller before this man arrived," shouted a man in the middle of the townspeople, raising his hand. "I will gladly lodge you and your company for as many nights as you desire."

A cheer went around the first floor of the hostel, and people quickly set to refreshing the bedding and fetching food. It seemed they planned to feed the entire port at a feast in Beatriz's honor.

While everyone was occupied, Beatriz used an old broom to sweep the scabs into the ashes of the hearth. Wiping her hands on her apron, she fished the plant out of the cookpot. Even holding it up to the light from the window, it didn't show any signs of having been used. The leaves were still as green, the petals just as springy as when St. Mary had tucked them behind Beatriz's ear in the dream. The plant wasn't even waterlogged.

"Ave Maria," Beatriz whispered. She stowed the plant in her apron pocket and went to help her pilgrim friends make beds.

VII.

After a long night of dancing and feasting, Beatriz slept on one of the upstairs bedrolls as if it had the softest mattress and hundreds of pillows. When the light through the windows advanced to her eyelids, she sat up to find that someone had left a richly embroidered red velvet gown at her feet. It reminded her of her life as the empress, and her hands caressed the soft fabric longingly. She didn't want to accept any further payment after what the people of Gythion had done for her, but the others had already gone downstairs, and she was alone.

"No harm in trying it on," muttered Beatriz. It took some time and concentration to lace herself up. When she finished, she felt so beautiful, she twirled around the long dormitory.

At the end of a spectacular flourish, she found herself face to face with the hospitaller's wife at the top of the twisting wooden staircase.

"I'm glad you like it," she said. "The tailor wanted to donate it to you."

"Oh, it's the most beautiful dress I've seen in a long time, but I can't accept it," protested Beatriz. "My healing services must be freely given, as they were granted to me."

"Consider it a loan while we wash your dress," she said, crossing to Beatriz's bedroll to fetch the garment. "Hmm, it has some old stains. It may take some time to work these out."

By the afternoon, other leprosy sufferers from around the Peloponnesus began to arrive. They crowded into the hostel and watched expectantly while Beatriz brewed two cookpots worth of the tisane with water her pilgrim friends had brought. She ladled the remedy to each leper individually in her velvet gown to the applause of people from the town.

Her pilgrim friends stared at her as if she were part of a miniature in a book of prayers, but it was far from the worst way she'd been gazed upon. It was no trouble to smile brightly and sincerely for hours on end. Afterward, she retrieved the plant from the cookpot and stashed it in the bag hidden under her overskirt.

At the end of two more days during which more and more lepers arrived with no sign of flagging, the leader of the pilgrims took Beatriz aside. He told her that they needed to move on in order to fulfill their promise to visit Jerusalem. She told him she would stay in Gythion a little longer, since there was so much work to do. They bade farewell in the port the following morning, and for the first time since the barren rock, Beatriz felt sad. They had been the first people who had treated her kindly, and it was unlikely she would see them again.

After a few more days in Gythion, the empress decided to move on to Athens. There, she could heal more people and most of them wouldn't have to travel as far. The Gythionites, who were becoming rich with the influx of visitors, were sorry to see her go. But it wasn't hard to find a captain willing to give her passage to Athens. In spite of having no money or anything to trade, her fame as a woman blessed by St. Mary made everyone her friend.

She spent a month in Athens and cured a thousand lepers. She moved on to Crete, then to Rhodes. She'd been healing in Paphos on Cyprus for only seven days when a group of men wearing the almost-forgotten uniforms of the Roman Imperial Guard, not suffering from leprosy, broke through the orderly line of twelve patients and interrupted the session.

"Are you the famous healer who cures lepers?" said the one in front.

His nearest companion punched him in the arm. "Of course she is, look at her!"

The first continued to address Beatriz. "You've been summoned to the court of the Emperor of Rome. We have an outbreak of leprosy that has reached into the palace to threaten the life of the emperor's beloved brother, and it is known that you are kind and will heal him and the rest of the city, besides."

"The emperor's brother?" Beatriz smiled. It seemed the Mother of God was giving everyone their just reward, even Felix. "Thank you for your flattering words. Please wait behind these poor, suffering souls. When I've finished here, I will speak with you."

The emperor's men threw their hands up in surprise. They probably weren't accustomed to waiting. They didn't seem to know how to make themselves smaller, and remained where they were, letting the afflicted wind around them as if they were the interruption in the imperial plans.

Beatriz ladled the tisane and let the sufferer take it into his hands, which shook with apparent age. Just as the first time, and the thousand times after, this patient drank it up with relish, and in the next instant, his sores fell to the floor.

The other sufferers who waited broke out into applause. The hostel staff were well accustomed, and a maid dutifully swept up the sloughed remains of the man's illness. The man himself embraced Beatriz with the gusto of a twenty-year-old, and she accepted his happiness as her own. The emperor's men, in contrast, stared at the scene with wide eyes.

"So you see, what you've heard about me is true," Beatriz said to them. "And you won't have to wait long. I'll be finished here presently."

They waited patiently and witnessed the wonder repeated eleven more times. The empress's conversation with them was formal and filled with mutual respect, but she didn't agree to go with them until she'd checked with the hospitaller and made certain that no more people with leprosy were expected to come soon.

Beatriz enjoyed a luxurious cabin on deck. They comfortably skirted the Greek Islands, such that the crew could bring Beatriz fresh meals nearly every day.

When they docked in a port city, the empress went ashore and asked if anyone suffering from leprosy was nearby. In this way, she cured many more people who had become ill and repented their sins, and the days passed quickly.

While they sailed, Beatriz read from a prayer book the grateful daughter of a man cured in Siphnos insisted she take. They worked their way up the coast of Greece and the south of the Italian Peninsula. They stopped for a few days in Messina on Sicily, and Beatriz wondered if it was similar to the Syracuse she hadn't been able to visit.

She insisted on stopping at every port between there and Ostia, because the plague of leprosy was fierce enough in the south, but also because, as the land became more and more familiar to her, she found more and more misgivings in her heart.

Since receiving the miraculous plant, people treated her better than when she had been empress. They never questioned her judgement and always did her bidding. Their attentions to her had a sincerity that had been lacking all of Beatriz's life. They weren't bowing and scraping before her because the emperor was by her side, but because she was finally doing good in the world. What did it mean that she was returning to Rome?

She had been the empress of this beautiful, civilized place, only to be sent off to die, then sold as a slave. Could she find the kindness in her heart to cure Felix, the man who'd set off that terrible chain of events? Watching the coastline with its fishing boats and seabirds slide by, she stroked the sprig St. Mary had given her in a dream. The blooms never wilted, the leaves never curled, no matter how long they spent pressed in her apron pocket, no matter how many cookpots of tisane she brewed. The plant was like St. Mary's infinite forgiveness and grace.

Beatriz wasn't at all certain she could be as merciful as the Mother of God. She paced the deck, unable to calm the chills that ran through her body faster and faster as the ship skimmed closer and closer to Ostia.

And then they were there. The ship slowed and eased next to a dock covered in algae with half the planks missing. Hardly any ships were in port, and those that were looked to be on the point of sinking. Piles of tangled nets cluttered the wharf, and mangy dogs and cats ran at the seagulls who picked apart rancid carrion of the sea. It was not the port Beatriz had left a little over a year previously. Her misgivings multiplied.

"Why is it like this? The port of Rome used to

reflect the empire's power and wealth," she asked one of the emperor's men.

"Ever since the emperor's brother fell ill, all taxes have gone to pay for treatments that have never worked. No one can convince the emperor to stop paying these physicians."

"I will accept no payment for my treatments, as you know. This port will soon prosper again." The port was a reflection of Felix's moral failings. Perhaps if Beatriz healed him, all of Rome would benefit. She would have to step in and bring Rome back to the glorious state she'd left it in before this neglect, before the emperor had stopped believing in her. She wrung her hands, oppressed by the weight of responsibility.

The imperial guards cleared the way to disembark, laying extra rails to cover the gaps. Even so, Beatriz allowed several soldiers to lead and try it out first. From the moment their feet hit the dock, a murmuring from inside the neglected buildings along the wharf became a swarm of people. They crowded the guards, who pushed them back with their shields. Beatriz looked at their faces and hands. They were all infected.

"Stand down. Let them through. I would speak with these gentle people," said Beatriz.

The guards fell away to the side, leaving no barrier between Beatriz and the people of the port. Many of them clambered over each other to reach her. Several were able to clasp her hands and plead something in a rush before they were pushed out of the way by others. When a demure woman who tried to hide the scars on her face with a linen veil was in front, Beatriz held up her hand. "Let this lady have her say."

When the crowd was finally silent, the woman took Beatriz's hand gently. "We had word from Terracina that the great lady who cures all lepers was headed to Rome, so we've all come."

"It's true, and I am that lady. Take me to a hospital with a cookpot or several, and plenty of fresh water, and I'll cure you all."

An uproar ensued, and the infected crowd made its chaotic way to the building that Beatriz used to know as the most elegant hostel at the port. Before she could follow them, an imperial guard held her back.

"Saintly lady, we must hurry to the imperial palace. We can't let the emperor's brother suffer longer than he has to."

"If he remains as I recall him, Lord Felix can hold out for a few more days. His is no more important or urgent than the cases of these children of God."

Behind her, the guards whispered in disbelief about her knowing the emperor's brother as she strolled to the hostel. Although the walls seemed to be falling apart, it was neither the worst nor the best place Beatriz had performed her cures. The cookpot was large, and there were plenty of people among the cured and their families who helped bring the water. Three days went by before Beatriz noticed the imperial guards pacing nervously. The fourth day, they tried to turn sufferers away at the door, but Beatriz simply brought the ladle out to them.

The fifth day, the first in line were Count Magnus and his brother, Rufus. The murderer was unrecognizable with his hands and face wrapped in linens, but even from the doorway, Beatriz knew those two men in whose house she had cared for a darling boy, had so recently been beaten, and from which she had been escorted away to die. The guards didn't bother them because of the count's rich clothing and noble bearing, and when they stepped inside, the empress dropped the first ladleful of tisane, spilling it on the hearth.

"Stay there, Rufus," the count told his brother at the door. He approached Beatriz, who knelt on the floor, wiping up the tisane with a rag. "I'm sorry if we were the cause of this spill. We can pay double, or triple, or anything you ask, if you cure my brother."

Beatriz turned her face to the count, but there was no recognition in his eyes. Had her appearance altered tremendously during her year of traveling and healing? Had St. Mary placed a spiritual blindfold over his eyes? Somehow, he didn't know who she was.

"I don't charge anything at all for my services," she said standing. "And your brother must come close if I'm to heal him. I'm not afraid." She said it hoping it would become true.

The shrouded form came forth, and stopped when there was only an arm's length between them. Beatriz observed the skin around Rufus's eyes, in dry gray patches and running red sores. If the disease was left untreated, he would soon lose his sight. But any pity Beatriz might have felt drowned in the knowledge that this man had murdered his tiny, innocent nephew and profited off what he supposed was her death.

"Remove your linen. I must examine your face," she said.

He raised his hands, and even through the wrappings, she could tell he was missing several fingers. It appeared he could hardly move the fingers he had. He lowered the cloth clumsily to lips that had receded to reveal a ghastly grin and a hole rimmed by rotting green flesh where there should've been a nose.

"This is the worst case I've ever seen," said Beatriz, blinking back tears of horror. "My tisane alone will not be enough." She looked at the count. "This man must cure his spiritual ills as well. Before he drinks from my ladle, he must confess his crimes, which must be legion."

"Anything, if you can save him. He's the only family I have, apart from my wife," said the count.

The leper grunted and covered his face. Beatriz supposed he couldn't speak very well.

"But may we be seated? He hardly made it here from the carriage," said Count Magnus.

"Of course." Beatriz pointed to a table with a bench in the far corner with room for many more than two. "Let him make his confession to you. I don't need to hear."

While the men murmured together, Beatriz cured the next sufferer. The more disease that sloughed off to the floor, the more hope was reflected in the count's face even as he listened to whatever Rufus mumbled. Before she'd cured two more, however, the count shrieked and collapsed to his knees.

"Evander! You killed my Evander, my only son." He wept into his hands. "To what gain?"

"Don't mind them. Drink up. It's good," the empress encouraged her patient.

"Beatriz!" shouted Magnus, and she looked over. But the count wasn't calling to her. He thought she was dead. "That poor, gentle lady, lost because of you. Why did I believe you instead of her?"

The count pummeled his fists into Rufus's legs, but it didn't seem he could feel the blows. "You truly deserve this punishment God has visited upon you."

Realizing he wasn't making Rufus suffer, the count stood and screamed into his hands. He rent his tunic from the neck and marched out of the inn. The line of sufferers made way, and when the count was gone, their silent stares turned to Rufus. He slumped over, burying what was left of his face in his arms.

Beatriz's patient had drunk and been cured, so she applauded to lighten the others' spirits, although her heart was a confusion of conflicting feelings.

When the last leper in line had left behind the signs of his illness, and Beatriz had swept his scars into the hearth, she removed the miraculous sprig from the cookpot and tucked it in her apron pocket. As St. Mary would want, she scooped up the last ladleful of tisane and carried it with both hands to the suffering pile of rotten flesh and linen that had once been the strong and handsome brother of the count.

"Drink," she said. "I see that you've confessed your sins at great cost to yourself. I must cure you."

She looked away as he pulled the linen from his face and poured the miraculous liquid into his gullet. When he dropped the ladle, she returned her gaze to him, expecting to see the handsome face of Evander's murderer. But those wild eyes stared back at her from a grotesque putrefied face, nearly the same as when he'd arrived.

She forced herself to examine his eyes, and they were no longer red, but none of his flesh had been restored, and none of the discoloration had flaked off. She picked up the ladle, and none of the tisane had spilled on the floor, so he must've drunk it all.

Rufus said something, indistinct because of his disfigurement. Beatriz asked him to repeat himself, and in the end, she understood that he was asking why he hadn't made a full recovery like the others.

"Your life has been spared because of your sincere confession, and the infection seems to have stopped its fatal progress. But I think your crimes were too great to be cured by my simple drink. Your deformity must bear witness to your crimes for all to see, so that you may never return to your evil ways."

Rufus surged from the bench, supporting himself as he could on the table. He didn't try to speak, but stared at Beatriz until finally she thought he must recognize her. His gaze held no malice, but resignation. Tears fell down his scarred cheeks. He pulled the linen back up to his eyes and headed for the door. He stumbled without the count's support, and Beatriz guessed he didn't have any toes.

She set to cleaning the cookpot, unable to deal with the contradictory emotions the pathetic figure provoked. Should she have brewed more tisane to see if it would help? He had done unspeakable things, but wasn't there a limit to what such suffering could teach him?

It wasn't for Beatriz to decide whether he was truly contrite or the type of judgment he deserved. "Ave Maria," she said, fingering the silky flower petals in her pocket.

One of the imperial guards came to stand in the doorway with his customary impatience. Beatriz acknowledged him with a sad smile.

"It's time to go to the imperial palace."

VIII.

The carriage in which the soldiers took Beatriz to the palace had soft cushions and no sign of hooks to tie someone down. She insisted the curtains be pulled back so she could view the city with its ruins. Even the new buildings seemed to have stopped construction in the middle.

The journey was the same one she'd taken to come and marry the emperor, but the landscape had changed. She knew she was different, too, but she felt the same trepidation she had on that first carriage ride. This time, there was no chaperone to hold her hand and stroke her hair. She fidgeted with the sprig in her pocket more and more, the closer they drew to the imperial palace.

They barely paused at the gate, as the guards

recognized their comrades and knew the urgency of their mission. Beatriz studied their serious faces as the carriage passed. She knew some of the men from her time in the palace, but they were changed, as well. There was none of the camaraderie or pride she remembered sometimes envying.

A guard helped Beatriz alight, and she felt grandiose in her red velvet gown, even as used as it was. The pages who came out to meet them kept their distance, but even from afar, they trembled obviously with fear. It seemed more basic than concern for the emperor's brother.

Beatriz approached one. He backed against the wall and turned his face away. She thought she recalled he'd come to wait upon the emperor shortly before Antoninus left for the crusade.

"Why are you so afraid?" she asked him. She guided his chin to face her, but just like the count and Rufus in the port, no recognition registered on his face.

Eying the imperial guards, the young man whispered so they wouldn't hear. "I've lost many of my comrades to the illness that afflicts the emperor's brother. When one of us can no longer work, they send in another of us. I'm afraid I'll be next to attend to him personally and clean his wounds."

Tears filled his eyes, and Beatriz saw all the hopes he may have had to marry and start his own family flow down his cheeks with them. She understood that she must help Felix, no matter what he'd done to her.

She couldn't let so many good Romans suffer any longer because of his villainy. She hoped the tisane would work sufficiently to help Rome return to its former glory, but that wasn't for her to decide.

"I'm here to cure the emperor's brother," she said for all to hear. "You have nothing to fear."

"It's true," said an imperial guard. "We've seen what this lady does with her blessed plant. So stop your sniveling."

The page wiped his tears and stood at attention, chastised. Beatriz smiled back at him as they headed to the throne room, trying to inject some hope into the now desolate palace.

She nearly forgot herself and strode ahead to the throne room. But familiar face after familiar face made no acknowledgement that they knew her, so she pretended she'd never been in the palace before. Her gasps of surprise at the shabby state of the furniture and walls probably seemed to be wonderment.

"You've never been anywhere so elegant before,

have you?" one of the guards whispered in her ear with too much familiarity.

She giggled in a way that could be interpreted to mean any number of things.

When they opened the door of the throne room and she saw her Antoninus, she was unable to say anything at all.

He sat crooked, uncomfortable on a throne he was born to occupy. His hair, which fell past his shoulders, was like a dingy gray veil that nearly obscured his sad eyes. If he'd ever looked like that while Beatriz lived at the palace, she would have taken him away from his duties and listened to him and held him tight until he found his strength again.

For a long moment, they gazed at each other wordlessly. He didn't recognize her. Their years of happiness together had been erased. As the reason for her visit registered, he began to grin and sit up straighter.

A guard tapped her shoulder. "Bow before the emperor."

Beatriz was quick to comply, to do anything but keep looking at this shell of Antoninus, but the emperor said, "Nonsense! If this is the miraculous lady who can cure my brother, let her stand before me as an equal."

She stood and was grateful to talk about the matter at hand.

He gestured at her regally. "Behold, cure my leprous brother, and I shall give you a great reward."

"I believe I can help your brother. If your Imperial Majesty will allow it, I would see the patient and talk with him."

"I can't let you risk it, dear lady," said the emperor. "Talk with the page who serves him about his symptoms."

"I must speak with him myself, and when the time comes, I must administer the tisane by my own hand. I have cured more than a thousand lepers and never been contaminated, for I am protected by the Mother of God."

"Very well," said Antoninus. "I will escort you and wait outside the chamber."

Beatriz was overwhelmed with memories as Antoninus walked beside her. It was as if the past five years had never taken place. They glided along the corridors confident in their unity and in their governance of the empire. She'd thought Felix would be staying in one of the many luxurious guest quarters for diplomats and foreign rulers. But they stopped before the door of her own bedroom.

With trepidation, she left the emperor and the

guards and stepped inside. The gilded armchair where she'd spent so many hours reading to her lady attendants was still on its platform, as if Beatriz had stepped out momentarily to dine or to greet an ambassador. The colorful pillows still softened every surface, and of course the colonnade still commanded a sweeping view of Rome.

The bed was still big enough for half the servants in the palace to sleep comfortably, but in it, a single masculine figure reclined, wrapped up in linen. No book of prayers to St. Mary or rosary was in his hand. Beatriz seemed to have interrupted him staring out at Rome with an empty expression.

"Who are you?" said Felix. "Where's my page? It's not time to change my linens." He sat up straight with a challenge in his eyes.

"I'm the lady who's come to cure you of your ailment," said Beatriz, feeling more disgust at his ridiculous lack of humility than she ever had looking at any leper's suffering. "You must let me see the affected areas so I can tell whether I'll be able to help you."

"Why should you be able to help me when the finest physicians in the entire empire have failed?" He brought his knees up to his chest defensively.

Beatriz leaned on a column like an old friend and

contemplated the most important city in the world, of which she had been the empress. "Because I'm not a physician. Because I'm protected by the Mother of God."

She charged to the bed and forced his knees and arms away from his face with divine ferocity. "And because I'm not doing it for you, but for all the Roman citizens whose lives you're ruining and wasting."

He struggled to return to his cocoon, but when he looked her in the eye, he seemed to know he was beaten. He went limp and let her lift the bandages from his hands, feet, and finally his face. His flesh was mottled with multicolored sores and rough scars. Beatriz didn't choose to linger looking at it, but no infection threatened his eyes or nose, and none of his fingers or toes were missing. Under that strange reptilian surface, she could still make out the aquiline features of this younger version of Antoninus. Compared to Rufus, Felix's malady looked almost comfortable. Was he redeemable, after all?

"Hmm," she said.

"What? What is it? Am I going to die?"

She considered letting him suffer in ignorance while she loosely replaced the bandages. She sighed.

"I've seen worse. Prepare yourself to save your own life."

She marched out the door unhurried, leaving his shouts of bewilderment behind her.

Once they'd closed the door, all the guards and especially the emperor gazed at her expectantly. She murmured only to Antoninus.

"Your brother will recover, but before I do anything for him, he must confess all his sins, exactly as he committed them."

"Of course," said the emperor, snapping his fingers at the nearest guard. "Fetch a priest."

Beatriz started again. "He must confess to the pope, and Your Imperial Majesty must be there to listen."

The emperor furrowed his brow the way he used to when Beatriz suggested something more complex than he'd anticipated. "Why must we call in the pope?"

"I've seen it in the nature of his wounds, Your Imperial Majesty. His sins are too grave for any other of God's intermediaries. Your Imperial Majesty must hear everything he says because some of your brother's sins have affected you, beyond the general effect he's had on the palace and even the entire empire."

Beatriz crossed her arms and looked into Antoninus's eyes as steadily as if she were the empress he didn't recognize.

"Well, what are you waiting for?" the emperor shouted at the guards. "Go to the papal palace immediately and request His Holiness's presence."

The guards looked at each other, and by silent agreement, ran down the corridor toward the exit together. Beatriz was alone with Antoninus.

She recalled the last time he'd spoken to her, ordering his new foreign guards to take her away and kill her. Did he think of that day? Did he ever question his decision? Had anyone else in the palace tried to tell him what had really happened? Or had Felix made sure to fill his mind with lie after lie until the emperor hardly had a true thought in his head anymore?

"His Holiness will probably come tomorrow, since I'm asking personally," said Antoninus. "In the meantime, I'll have someone ready you a guest suite to sleep in."

Standing outside her rightful quarters, where many had been the times Beatriz had coquettishly invited the emperor to spend the night, nostalgia washed over her. Her body reacted to the half-remembered longing with a coughing fit.

The emperor reached out to comfort her, but stayed his hand and took a step back. "Are you sure you can't catch what Felix has?"

"It's nothing, Your Imperial Majesty," choked Beatriz. "It's only that I'd prefer to sleep with female servants, perhaps cooks or maids, whoever lives here, than to stay by myself. I've been traveling, dedicated to helping lepers, and have become accustomed to that sort of company."

"Very well," said Antoninus, though he sniffed at the strangeness of her request. "I do want you to be comfortable and at your best tomorrow. And since you're used to conviviality, I hope you'll join me for dinner. I'd love to learn more about this wondrous lady who can alleviate my brother's suffering."

Beatriz's mind raced. "Your Imperial Majesty means St. Mary, not I, and I'm afraid since it's Saturday, her day, I must fast until tomorrow. You did say the pope would come tomorrow?"

"Count on it," said Antoninus. "Perhaps after the curing, we can all dine together in celebration."

"Of course," Beatriz lied. She knew she could never sit through a meal with the emperor without breaking down, and certainly would never willingly attend a dinner with Felix again.

They parted ways with ceremonious bows near

the kitchen, where Beatriz was to seek out a scullery maid who could show her their dormitory.

But the empress kept thinking how she used to stand there discussing menus for suppers with diplomats and foreign heads of state and found it impossible to enter the kitchen. The longer she stood there, the worse her head hurt. She followed a strong pull outside the palace. The guards at the gate crossed their staffs in front of her.

"Please let me go. I'll come back to cure the emperor's brother," Beatriz said. "I can't stay here in this luxury when I know there are good Romans who need my help."

"We can't let you go," said a guard. "We must keep an eye on you at all times, by the emperor's direct orders."

"Come with me, then. You can see my work, and if something were to happen to me, you could decide whether to report to the palace or just go into hiding to avoid the emperor's wrath." She laughed nervously, but it seemed to convince them.

The tall one guided her through neighborhoods she'd never visited before. Filth ran freely down the sides of the streets, and people were too busy hawking wares or trudging home to notice. Those with the worst luck of all sat among the refuse with their hands out, moaning plaintively, not even using words to say what they needed.

It wasn't long before Beatriz saw the telltale sores on the hands of one of the downtrodden souls.

"Stop," she said before the guard slipped away without knowing he'd left her behind.

He turned around and looked on with curiosity and not a little revulsion.

The woman was dressed in scraps, and her eyes were white. Beatriz didn't know if the blindness was a complication from her leprosy, but it didn't matter. She was defenseless, and the only one who could help her was Beatriz.

The empress held out her hand. "Follow my voice, dear lady, and take my hand. I'm taking you to an inn where I can cure you."

"I've heard tell of the lady who cures untouchables," said the woman, clearing her throat. "Are you that lady? Have you come to us at last?"

"I am that lady, sent by St. Mary, and I can cure all who believe in her."

The woman found Beatriz's hand and hoisted herself up. "Please take us to the nearest hostel," Beatriz requested of the guard. She wasn't able to hear his affirmative reply, because the leprous woman started shouting.

"Hey, everybody! The lady who cures lepers is here! Bring your loved ones! Bring lepers who owe you money! We're all getting cured!"

"Shut up!" shouted the guard, raising his hand against her.

Beatriz stayed him. "It's all right. I'm here to cure. I might as well cure them all."

They progressed through the twisting streets, and the woman continued to shout, drawing people out of buildings and alleyways Beatriz hadn't even noticed.

"How many people are hiding and suffering?" she whispered. She couldn't bear the thought, and avoiding such tragedy in the City of Rome impelled her to the inn right behind the guard. The innkeeper abandoned the building as soon as he caught sight of the ailing mob following the beautiful lady and the imperial guard.

Of course, the water took its time boiling in the enormous pot on the hearth. The lepers piled in through the door and the windows, and the guard tried to keep them back with his staff.

"Patience, patience!" said the empress, chuckling to herself. "No one will go untreated. You've waited this long. You can wait a few more minutes."

No one argued when the blind woman went first,

and with the tisane from the still-fresh plant, she regained her sight. It was enough to give everyone hope and a little of the patience Beatriz needed from them. The second person cured was a priest, and Beatriz had him set up in the corner so the sufferers could talk to him first and receive the tisane fully confessed.

The empress quickly lost track of the number of people she cured. Volunteers helped her keep the cookpot full of water and the fire stoked, but she personally ministered the tisane to every last patient. Finally, the clump of people waiting thinned out, and the former lepers started to feel like stopping the celebration and surprising their families back at home when the sun broke through a crack in the wooden shutters.

The priest helped Beatriz put the hostel back in order, and when they were done, he said, "Would you like me to wake him up for you, blessed child?"

The empress observed the imperial guard, who had slumped over a table, his face buried in his arms. "Yes, thank you," she told the priest.

She reached into the cookpot for the plant in order to tuck it back into her apron, but hesitated. The sprig was still whole and green, but the biggest of the white flowers had left several wilted petals in the bottom of the pot. She turned the plant over in her hand, and nothing else seemed amiss. She wasn't sure what the loss of the petals meant, and staying up all night was catching up with her. She might have remained frozen in that spot for several hours if the guard hadn't started shouting.

"St. Mary, save me! We must return to the palace. The emperor will be looking for you, and if my companion at the gate can't tell him where you are…"

Beatriz stuck the plant in its customary place. "Of course. I'm ready. Let's go now."

They hurried through the narrow streets, bustling with morning activity. People smiled and waved at her. They must've been former lepers, or their families. She couldn't tell anymore. Beatriz felt dizzy, battered by the noise and smells of people shouting, cooking, and throwing refuse into the street. She clung to the guard's arm, and he managed to guide her to a cleaner, quieter neighborhood. From the middle of the street, she could see the path up to the imperial palace, where Felix awaited the same treatment she'd given to every poor soul who confessed all night long.

She should keep going, just a little while longer. It would all be over soon. She collapsed on the compacted earth.

IX.

Beatriz awoke in her own bedroom in the palace. She'd been laid on cushions next to the colonnade, and when she lifted her head, all of Rome spread out before her. Perhaps the past five years had been a long, vivid nightmare. Her headache and queasiness indicated she might've feasted on something very rich too soon before bed.

The page she remembered from long ago stood up from a nearby cushion. "Are you all right?" he asked. "They brought you in unconscious. The emperor thought this was the best place for you, so I've been watching to make sure you're all right. Are you?"

"I'll be fine," Beatriz murmured.

Her hand darted instinctually to her apron pocket.

The miraculous plant was still there. So she had indeed lived through unimaginable trials and nearly died. But then she had been blessed by St. Mary. She pulled the sprig out, and in the morning light, she saw that the largest flower was completely wilted, and some of the smallest ones had lost a few petals, as well.

Would it be potent enough to cure Felix? She shuddered to think what could happen to Rome if it didn't. For herself, she hardly cared any longer. She sighed and renewed her trust in the Queen of Heaven.

She stood, catching herself on a column, shooing off the page, and managed to pocket the plant. Felix was sitting up in the bed as if he hadn't moved since her examination the previous day.

"What, did you get drunk last night? Tell me the truth, you're from the brothel downtown, sent by someone I owe money to, and you're going to poison me with that plant."

Beatriz didn't want to dignify his remark with a response, but a higher impulse told her he needed to prepare to cleanse his spirit.

"Those are the kinds of thoughts you're having right before His Holiness the Pope comes to take your confession?" She walked dismissively to the door. The page hurried to open it for her.

Ten guards stood at attention in the passage. The number seemed excessive to Beatriz.

"What a relief, dear lady!" said the guard from the previous night. "I carried you to the palace. You had me worried."

"I thank you for taking care of me," said Beatriz. "You may tell the emperor I've woken."

"He's receiving the pope now," said the guard. He sent one of the others to the throne room to deliver the message. "They'll probably come immediately."

"Perfect," sighed Beatriz. The Blessed Mother had made sure everything happened at the right moment. The page closed the door against the thrashing and profanities coming from the bed, and they waited in silence for just a few moments.

Their animated chatter pealed through the passageway before they took the turn. The emperor headed the parade, with the papal retinue following. Although he was surrounded by cardinals in red capes, His Holiness stood out with his tall triangular papal miter, vermillion with golden trim. Peering beyond the ostentation, Beatriz saw jolly, gleaming eyes and a tidy gray beard. As they approached, she dropped to her knees, and the guards and page imitated her.

"You must be the wonderous woman who cures lepers. You may stand in my presence. From what I've been told, you are doubtless blessed by the Holy Mother herself." He put out his bejeweled hand, and Beatriz kissed a ring, then stood, dusting off her knees.

"The emperor's brother is as ready as he'll ever be, Your Holiness. Please enter at your leisure." Beatriz motioned to the page to open the door.

"I admit to being hesitant to stand too close to a leper, dear child," said the pope.

"Thank you for your frankness, Your Holiness. It's a large room, and you can easily avoid touching the patient. But there's no cause for fear. I know St. Mary would never permit the patient's vileness to infect Your Holiness. Just as she has protected me, you will leave this palace intact."

She extended her arm toward the open door, through which they could see Felix, still writhing, on the bed. The pope remained next to Beatriz, rotating the rings on his fingers. Beatriz wasn't sure what else to do.

"Never doubt what this woman says, Your Holiness," said Antoninus. "I've heard stories of the miraculous recoveries she worked at the port. This woman is beyond suspicion."

Beatriz bit her lip. Otherwise, she would've laid into her husband, demanding to know where this faith in her was in the face of Felix's lies five years previously.

"May I speak, Your Imperial Majesty and Your Holiness?" Beatriz's guard from the previous night requested, remaining on his knees. Both men nodded. "Last night, I witnessed this kind lady touch more than one hundred lepers before my very eyes and cure each one. And that was before I fell asleep. She's been doing this for a year or more, and has never fallen ill. No one has anything to fear." He bowed his head humbly.

"Will you join us, child?" said the pope.

"I don't need to hear what he has to say, Your Holiness. I'll prepare the tisane so it will be ready when he is." She bowed deeply. When she'd witnessed both men enter the room and stand in the colonnade, facing a terrified Felix, she walked deliberately down the passage, accepting no company.

In the kitchen, she let a scullery maid set a cookpot to boil. The woman tried to make conversation, and Beatriz maintained it out of courtesy. But thinking of worldly, fleeting things made the empress see as if through a veil of decrepitude, and the impatience almost choked her.

When the water was ready, the maid ladled some into a goblet. A leaf fell off the plant as Beatriz placed it inside. She curtseyed to the maid, picked the leaf up from the floor, and carried the goblet by the stem, careful not to spill it as she returned through the passage.

She heard the emperor's shouting before the turn.

"Ah, God! How can this be? No one has ever heard of greater treason than this!"

Antoninus stood in the open doorway, flailing his arms. Beatriz saw the pope behind him, near the colonnade, making signs of absolution. It was done.

The emperor tore at his velvet robe. None of the guards made a move.

"Your Imperial Majesty, what happened?" asked Beatriz.

"I never knew he committed so many sins! But what matters is that now he says the empress never betrayed me, never tried to seduce him when I was in Jerusalem. My Beatriz! I sent my beloved empress to her death because of the lies that cretin told me…"

Whimpers came out of the mouth she'd kissed so happily for so many years, and tears streamed down his face, still handsome covered by a white beard. The sight would've broken Beatriz's heart if only it hadn't been shredded beyond repair every time she'd thought of Antoninus over the past five years.

Beatriz wiped at her own cheek. "Your Imperial Majesty, it's time for me to cure your brother. I'm obliged to use the gift St. Mary granted me. Afterward, you may mete out any punishment you desire. But let him face his fate whole in body. And... I have news of Empress Beatriz."

The emperor stopped his desperate movements, though his robe was already in tatters. "Beatriz? Is she alive?"

"I'll tell you afterward." She lifted the goblet with both hands to remind him of her duty. "Please let me through."

Antoninus gathered himself to the side of the door frame. Beatriz stepped over the shreds of cloth and nodded deeply at the pope, who returned the acknowledgment. She approached the bed, and Felix sat up defiantly.

"Oh, you're going to cure me now? How much good can it do me, when my brother's going to have me executed, anyway?"

"You may be surprised," said Beatriz. "But that's none of my concern. Drink."

His bandages swiped her fingers as he grasped the goblet stem. "Tell me truly: this is poison, isn't it?"

"No," Beatriz said, unable to keep herself from rolling her eyes.

"Drink, son," said the pope from the colonnade. "You must enjoy good health in order to carry out the penance I'm imposing on you."

Felix blinked as if deciding which fate was worse.

"I'm sure I can find someone to force you," said Beatriz.

Antoninus came to stand next to Beatriz. "I'll force you myself if you don't drink, Felix. You owe that much to Rome and to me."

Felix tipped the goblet more gently than Beatriz would have, dribbling tisane over his scarred lips. Lifting his head, he spoke in disbelief. "Even if it's poison, it tastes irresistible." He gulped the rest of the drink down until the miraculous plant fell out, hitting his nose on its way to the bedsheet.

Beatriz rescued the plant, stifling a sob of despair. It was a hazy memory of the plant St. Mary had tucked behind her ear, shriveled and unnaturally dry, with no flowers or any hint that there had ever been blooms on the stalk at all. The empress stood unmoving, astonished by the understanding that Felix had been her last patient.

She might've walked out of the room without speaking to anyone, but Antoninus touched her arm.

"Dear lady, gaze upon the miracle you've wrought!"

Felix was laughing as he stripped off his linen bandages, adding them on top of the diseased skin that had sloughed off him. Beatriz was thankful to think they would burn the sheets. His face was fresh and new, once again a younger version of her beloved Antoninus. If he wanted to, he could walk out of the palace and seduce any woman, command the respect of any man. Given Rufus's partial healing at the port hostel as well as the state of the plant, his recovery surprised Beatriz as much as everyone else.

But she wasn't one to question St. Mary's use of her power.

The guards and cardinals rushed into the room, celebrating. The pope kissed Beatriz's hands, calling her a saint.

Antoninus took her aside. "Thank you, kind lady. How may I reward you for my brother's miraculous recovery? Remember that I'm the Emperor of Rome. I can grant you anything you please."

"I will accept no payment for your brother's cure," replied Beatriz, "because I didn't work this miracle. It is the work of the Mother of God. We must keep her at the front of our minds, always, if we are to survive the trials this life tests us with."

Beatriz took Antoninus's hands in hers, but

dropped them again to stop the rush of emotions the touch provoked. He put them together in prayerful acknowledgement of Beatriz's wisdom. She wiped the tears flowing down her cheeks. She couldn't look into her husband's eyes, knowing what was about to happen.

"Your brother, as handsome as he is, has a soul as ugly as an ostrich."

At her words, Felix jumped out of the empress's bed and charged toward her. The imperial guards seized him and stopped him from touching her. Everyone in the room was going to hear what she said next.

"Now it can do no harm to tell you that I am the one to whom Felix did the greatest wrong, as he confessed. I swear it by the God of the True Cross." She held her hand up and closed her eyes in pledge.

"Beatriz?" said the emperor. He took her face in his hands, and she witnessed recognition blossom in his eyes. "My empress! It is you!"

He moved to embrace her, but Beatriz backed away holding her arm out. "No."

"Felix will never darken this palace again," Antoninus hurried to explain.

"I'll send him away to do the penance His Holiness has imposed. We can live just as we used to, before I left for the crusade, before I called my false and traitorous brother to Rome."

He pulled her hands away from her face, where she was catching copious tears. "Don't you remember how happy we were?" he pleaded.

She strode to the colonnade and watched Romans going about their business. "I'm afraid that now that my healing powers have come to an end, people will start treating me just as deplorably as before. There have always been men who were so moved by my beauty that my nobility and learning meant nothing to them. From now on, I wish to serve St. Mary, who is light, for she will never fail me."

"Would you enter a convent, my child?" asked the pope.

Beatriz nodded. "That would be an excellent start, Your Holiness. Do you know a holy place that would accept me?"

"Any convent would be glad to count you among their devotees. But I'm thinking of one in particular dedicated to St. Mary where you could be happy for the rest of your life."

"I would sleep there tonight, if they'll have me," said Beatriz.

The pope gestured at one of the cardinals, and he made a dramatic bow and exited.

"Is he going to the convent to advocate for me, Your Holiness? I'd like to go with him," said the empress.

"No!" shouted the emperor. He darted to Beatriz's feet and held onto her ankles. "Please don't go! I mourned you all these years, and now you're back, only to leave me again? Please stay in the palace. Give me a chance to win you back!"

His grip was surprisingly weak. Beatriz was able to step out of it, and he didn't try to grab her again, but lay on the floor weeping.

"I can never live in this palace. I'm not the woman I was when I lived here with you as your wife. I've seen too much suffering, survived infamy and physical attacks too many times. I'm sorry." She picked up her hem and ran to catch up with the cardinal before her spirit weakened.

In the convent, Beatriz worked and prayed. She traded her red velvet gown for a nun's habit with an underdress of sackcloth. Antoninus visited her daily, and in an alcove of the cloister, she listened to the rustling leaves and her husband's news of the world while she embroidered silk pillows.

She enjoyed hearing how Rome was recovering from the economic strain Felix had inflicted. Together they read letters from their daughter and son, and Beatriz was pleased when they expressed their agreement with her decision to enter the convent. Antoninus often asked her advice, and she responded with distant equanimity. She knew he was trying to tempt her to return to the world with power and the love they'd once shared, and she let him think he had a chance, because it seemed to lighten his spirit.

He told her what they'd done with Felix, but she was so uninterested, she didn't even listen. She was too busy thinking about what needed to be done in the scriptorium, where her literacy in several languages pleased the Mother Superior.

What most interested her about the convent was a small cell off the main altar. It could be entered through a doorway in the cemetery, and had a small window at eye level both on the side and cut into the church's apse. From there, she could see the figure of St. Mary with her Child clearly, albeit from the side. It had a bench that could double as a bedframe and a lower area in front of the apse window where Beatriz could imagine herself praying. It would be wonderful to live there for the rest of her days, entirely dedicated in spirit and body to St. Mary.

The next time Beatriz was alone with the Mother Superior in the scriptorium, she asked how long it had been since the convent had hosted an anchoress.

"Blessed Sor Florinda was called home to the Lord about ten years ago." She squinted at Beatriz. "Are you thinking of taking her place?"

"If I may," said Beatriz demurely.

The Mother Superior laughed. "The convent always benefits from an anchoress, but you should be in no rush to spend the rest of your life in that cell."

"I understand I must be examined before the confinement ceremony. I'd like to start the questioning process as soon as possible."

"Indeed, anyone who looks at you would say you're far too beautiful to become an anchoress," said the Mother Superior. "We'll need to be careful they don't lock you up somewhere else because they think you're a lunatic."

The Mother Superior must've told the emperor what was happening, because before Beatriz met with the bishop even once, Antoninus barreled into the cloister, demanding she be questioned by no less than the pope.

"Perhaps he can show you the error in your idea. Beatriz, Rome needs you. You must return to the palace. I can't lose you."

She'd long tried to think of a way to soften the

blow, but it was finally time to tell her husband where he'd erred.

"You lost me the moment you callously sent me off to be violated and killed without even listening to my self-defense. It took me years to understand, but I know now that in that moment, you demonstrated that you cared for your brother's words more than for the happy years we spent together, the good advice I'd given you, and the children I bore you. I can't sacrifice any more of myself for you. The Mother of God is a much kinder mistress."

Unable to comprehend Beatriz, Antoninus still held on to hope, and sent His Holiness, anyway. The pope was glad to meet with Beatriz, whom he always addressed as "blessed."

Over the course of the following year, they met ten times, strolling in the garden or huddling in the cloister for warmth, and one time, formally in the confessional.

Beatriz kept herself from crying out with impatience by acquiring a desk for the cell she already thought of as hers so she could keep working for the scriptorium and read letters from her children after her confinement. She also made heavy oak shutters for the window with her own hands, and began closing off the door with large stones she hauled in from the forest and plaster some of the nuns had shown her how to make.

She felt a little selfish, making the tiny space comfortable for only herself. But seeing how pleased the abbess was to have an anchoress again eased her mind. The abbey would receive more donations from patrons who wished the saintly woman in the cell to pray for their souls or their deceased loved ones. Such donations would likely double or triple the cost of Beatriz's modest food rations. People would still come to her window, tell her their troubles, and ask for blessings. It wasn't only a retreat from the world, but a way to give back that would keep Beatriz safe from physical and spiritual harm. She let herself anticipate the day she would enter the cell definitively with uncomplicated joy.

After their tenth meeting, Beatriz and the pope found Antoninus waiting for them in the cloister. Everyone made appropriate reverences, and the pope spoke first.

"I'm sorry, Your Imperial Majesty. There's nothing I can do. The Blessed Empress has told me how you sent her to her death without giving her a chance to confess, how a little boy she cared for was murdered in the bed next to her, and how she was abandoned on a rock in the middle of the

Mediterranean when she refused to accede to the gross desires of the crew of a Syrian ship. St. Mary has been her only friend in all of this, and even so, the Blessed Empress had to endure a year of traveling and seeing only illness and decay wherever she went. I've already discussed her case with the cardinals, and no one has ever seen anyone so spiritually ready to reject the world."

Beatriz smiled, but when she looked at Antoninus, he was weeping.

"I'll take care of you. It's the least I can do. The Imperial Crown will see to your physical needs in perpetuity." The emperor buried his head in his hands and stumbled blindly out of the cloister.

He returned a month later, when the pope said the last mass Beatriz would hear in the chapel. He sat in the back and never tried to approach Beatriz. He joined the pope, cardinals, and nuns as just one more witness at the door of the cell.

Beatriz knelt before His Holiness and received his blessing. Making the sign of the cross, she pledged, "I will never again lead a worldly life, nor wear silken cloth, nor gray squirrel fur. I will now seal myself within this cell and renounce the world forevermore."

She slipped inside the cell through the slit she'd left in the doorway. The nuns laid the final stones and plastered them in place, singing Gaude Virgo the whole time.

Beatriz sat on the bench and watched the ray of light become thinner until it was no more, and the singing stopped.

She closed the shutters and sat quietly in semidarkness.

Without the responsibilities of an empress or the tutor of a young boy.

Without the pressure of stares and rough hands on her person.

Without the duty to ceaselessly cure unfortunate people who clamored for relief.

For the first time, Beatriz felt unadulterated peace.

She felt a light within her. It grew year upon year. The people who brought her food and water or work for the scriptorium remarked on it. Those who arrived at her window seeking advice or a blessing trusted in it for many years, until the day she left to join St. Mary.

Did you enjoy this book? If so, please leave a phrase or two of a review on your favorite book platform for other readers to find. The author will be so grateful!

Our Lady's Troubadour offers ten more miraculous medieval stories with danger, excitement, and happy endings inspired by the *Cantigas de Santa Maria.* It's available everywhere in hardcover, paperback, and ebook from Encircle Publications (2021).

The author is happy to hear from you via her website: www.jessicaknauss.com.

Cantiga 5, page 1

Cantiga 5, page 2

The Author

J. K. Knauss grew up in Northern California and lives in Spain. In between, she's resided in Massachusetts, Oregon, Iowa, Leeds (England), Rhode Island, Pennsylvania, Arizona, Georgia, Illinois, North Carolina, and Granada, Córdoba, Sevilla, and Salamanca, Spain. She's worked as a librarian and a teacher of Spanish and English as well as an editor at small presses. She now does freelance bilingual editing. No matter where she's been, she's had two abiding loves: books and Spain. They culminated in her PhD in medieval Spanish literature and now in a burgeoning historical fiction career.

Visit her website, www.JessicaKnauss.com.

Also by J. K. Knauss

Our Lady's Troubadour
(Encircle Publications, 2021)

"What are you doing, Doña Auria?" shouted Manrique.

Auria straightened and held the Virgin and Child out to the squire. "The Moorish army must see who we have on our side."

Manrique gasped and crossed himself, then gingerly grasped the image by the arms.

Auria nodded at an archer, who made way for Manrique. The squire placed the Blessed Mother squarely on the edge of the battlement, where she would be visible all the way in the Kingdom of

Granada. From behind, Auria thought her hand looked less like a blessing than a gesture of military or royal domination.

"Let's see what she does." Manrique pulled all fourteen soldiers back from their posts.

A hush fell over the castle again, but it must only have been in Auria's mind, because the ladder landing between the merlons must've made a terrific clatter, and the first Moorish soldier who set foot on the battlement worked his mouth feverishly as he gestured at his fellows, so he must've been shouting.

[. . .]

Seven Noble Knights
(**Encircle Publications, 2020**)

Propelled by his lady's intensity, Little Page's stumpy legs carried him into the kitchen and then to the slaughterhouse. More quickly than Justa expected, he darted out again holding a cucumber in front of himself so as not to stain his fine tunic with the sludgy, reeking red-brown blood. The cucumber had been peeled in the kitchen and become engorged when Little Page scraped it along the inside of the bucket. The brothers saw him approaching and stopped their playing. Their voices carried to where Justa was standing with Doña Lambra.

"Do you suppose Doña Lambra's sent us something to eat?" asked Suero.

"I hope so," said Gonzalo. "Food can't come too soon for me."

Before their expectant eyes, Little Page ran. When his aim was true, he hurled the cucumber with all his might and hit Gonzalo squarely in the chest with it. Little Page didn't wait for the reaction, but turned and ran back toward Doña Lambra. The six brothers howled with laughter and the goshawk flapped its wings and squawked until Suero took it back. Blood had splattered over the bird and Gonzalo's chest and breeches, ruining them.

"You shouldn't be laughing. If this had happened to any of you, I wouldn't rest until you were avenged. He was proving he could wound and kill me if he wanted to. Stop laughing!" Gonzalo splashed water in a vain attempt to clean himself.

[...]

We All Fall Down
(Alhambra Press, 2020)

The Moors in Sevilla may have been our mortal enemies, but I can't fault anything they built in this city. The narrow streets provide relief from the unrelenting sun. […] My room in the Christian part of the palace has elegant vaulted ceilings and colorful painted tile walls, but whenever I'm allowed, I like to come to the old quarters, where Almohad hands crafted delicate arcs and curlicues into the plaster and channeled calming currents like brooks across the floor.

It's a beautiful prison.

[…]